Cover art by Derrick Gallagher

Books by Christopher woods
<u>Soulguard Series</u>
Soulguard
Soullord
Bloodlord
Rash'Tor'Ri
Freedom's Prophet
Freedom's Challenge (Forthcoming)

<u>This Fallen World Novellas</u>
This Fallen World
Broken City
Power Play (Forthcoming)

Freedom's Prophet
Christopher Woods

Cover Art by
Derrick Gallagher

Prologue

I held her hand as she screamed in pain.

"Push, Baby," I said.

She squeezed my hand just before everything went crazy. Her body jerked with spasms, and the hospital equipment went crazy with alarms.

"Dear God," one of the nurses mumbled as they furiously began working on my wife.

The doctor looked at my pale face, "It will pass, Mr. Hughes. She will be alright."

But it didn't pass and she was, most definitely, not alright. It was several minutes before the doctor began to work furiously to stabilize Jeanie.

"Prep for surgery," these words were the last I heard as they pushed me back out of the room.

This was the day I lost all that I held dear. I lost my wife, and my newborn son.

They say that your life flashes before your eyes when you die. I didn't see all of my life, just a small piece. Why did it have to be the most painful moment that I had to relive, as the blast from the exploding gateway rolled over me? Perhaps because that single moment in my life, sent me down a completely different path than the one I had planned to travel with her.

The pain of that moment sent me to a Marine recruiter, instead of back to the classroom where I taught American History. It sent me down the path of a soldier to fight in Korea, and later in Viet Nam. Viet Nam, where I was recruited to join the group of warriors that saved our lives from the many nightmares that were toying with us in the jungle.

Why didn't I get to relive the day I met a kid in Montana, who had a fire burning inside of him that drew those around him to follow? Or any number of days following that, where I worked with that kid as he grew to a man.

Perhaps because I didn't die, there, in that explosion. It certainly felt like I died, as the fires burned my flesh. I was Pulling strongly, and the Source was healing my injuries, but not enough to save me. In the middle of that fire, I had felt a cold envelope me as the gateway slipped over me. Then there was blackness.

Chapter 1

I heard fragments of sentences in the darkness, as my body felt a cooling sensation rising from my feet up my legs.

"...exhibits some of the traits..."

A second voice,"...unknown results..."

"Prime left explicit instructions..." yet another voice added.

"Perhaps...close enough..."

"Then we will try," the first voice answered.

My awareness slipped away, once again. When I started awake, I couldn't see clearly. Realizing I was completely immersed in liquid was a shock, considering I wore no sort of facemask. I was, literally, breathing the stuff. I jerked and a voice came from my left ear.

"Calm yourself," it said. "The liquid you are breathing will not harm you. It is an oxygen rich formula that helps you heal on the inside. You inhaled some of the fire as the portal destructed. Remain still, and breathe normally. Let the fluids heal you. We will talk soon enough about where you are. I am administering a sedative to help keep you calm, but it is not working."

I centered on myself as the focusing techniques I had learned instructed. First the heartbeat.

THUMP-THUMP, THUMP-THUMP.

Next breathe in and out. It felt weird with the liquid instead of air, but I could feel my lungs saturated with oxygen. I could feel the energy from that saturation flowing through my veins.

"I am increasing the sedative levels," the voice added.

I shook my head.

"That is a negative?"

I nodded.

"And that is a positive. I have seen your kind use that gesture," the voice continued. "Perhaps the excess presence of the energies from the Nexus keeps the sedatives from working."

The Nexus sounded a lot like the Source to me, so I nodded.

"I see," the voice said. "I have never had the chance to observe one with the amount of Nexus energies flowing into them that you possess. Combined with the recent changes, it is hard to foresee what may come for you in the future."

Changes? I wondered what he meant by that.

"It seems you have a greater speed of recovery than anyone else I have ever encountered."

"As if we had encountered anyone in Millennia," a second voice added.

"Be quiet," the first voice answered.

"Oh, now you don't want to hear us," the voice returned. "Now that you have found a pet."

"Enough from you..."

The speaker that was broadcasting to me shut down, and I assumed the two guys were arguing. I chuckled, which felt decidedly strange immersed in the liquid.

I shook my head, and focused on my body. The blood flowing through my veins... the pulling in and out of my lungs... my heartbeat...and gently, began to Pull from the Source into myself. The boy had shown me a few tricks about this sort of thing. You could tell when there was too much, and you would have to stop. But small amounts would help in the healing process.

"What is happening?" the voice was back and it sounded a bit frantic. "Why are the Nexus energies growing? Are you doing this?"

I nodded.

"You can draw more energy from the Nexus?"

"I nodded."

"Then those changes may indeed be more important than I had previously calculated."

I shrugged.

"Sensors show that the healing has sped up by a factor of fifty. Astonishing."

Welcome to the Soulguard, buddy.

"Can you do more?"

I really wasn't feeling any build up in my body, which was surprising. That familiar feel of energy was there, but not the bite of the fire that accompanies it.

I Pulled a little harder. There was a noticeable growth in the levels of energy, but still no burn from the fire. What the hell?

"Amazing! Healing has sped up by a factor of three thousand, and forty-two."

Were these the changes he had been talking about? I'd seen the Boss Pull massive amounts of power into himself. Or was the tank of fluid causing my ability to hold an increased amount of power?

I stopped Pulling. I didn't feel like I should risk it with my newfound second chance at life, wherever I was at. I could bust out of the tank at any time, but I could feel the healing going on inside of my body. There would be time for that later if the need arose.

"It is interesting," another voice added.

"Shh," the first one returned as the speaker cut out.

I focused again on what was happening inside of me, and did what many trained soldiers do when waiting for the time to take action, I closed my eyes. There would be time for learning about where I was after I could get out of the tank. The size of the explosion was enough to convince me that there was substantial damage. There wasn't any technology I knew of that worked like this, so I assumed I was on one of the other planets, probably the Kresh home world. It was the one with the gates connected to our own.

I didn't know who was behind the voices I heard. They had an odd sound to their voices, and they all had spoken English...

I opened my eyes for a moment as uncertainty settled over me. Had it been English? When I concentrated on the conversation, I wasn't sure. But how could it not have been English? I understood it, perfectly.

Another thing to find out when I was free of the tank. I closed my eyes again, and slowly sank into a meditative state that rested the body, as my mind focused on each part of it. It was a technique I had learned that would allow one to sleep in any situation. When the body was in full rest, the mind could do so as well.

Chapter 2

I awoke when I felt the liquid around me start to move. The current was new, and I could feel the fluid flowing past my feet toward a drain. This part would probably be uncomfortable. I had heard of deep sea divers using a fluid to breathe before, and I understood the transition could be nasty.

The fluid dropped past my eyes.

"You will need to cough the fluid from your lungs when it drops below your mouth," the voice said.

I was concentrating on it this time, and I was sure it wasn't English. But I couldn't stay focused on that, as my body had its natural reaction to the presence of air around it. My chest heaved and fluid erupted from my lungs. I tried to breathe in only to heave more fluid out. Then I sucked in one tortured breath of air.

Deep coughs followed, but I had passed that transition point, and felt the cool flow of air come into my lungs. The glass of the tube lifted, and I staggered forward, seeing my reflection in the shiny surface of the wall opposite me. My right side was scarred from burns on both my arm and leg. Also the right side of my torso from where I had been holding my arm up over my face was mottled with scarring and new tissue.

The rest should have been scarred as well, but it was a healthy pink color of new skin.

"Unfortunately, your accelerated healing had already created the scarring you see there on your right side. I was able to heal all the rest that your abilities had not already attempted."

I looked around, but there was no one in sight. The voice had sounded so close.

"Where are you?" I asked.

"I am all around you."

"What? What about the others?"

"There are no others here," the voice said.

I frowned, "Have it your way. I'm not going to hurt you. Come on out so I can meet the one who saved my life."

"I am part of this facility... Your name please?"

"Rictor... Rictor Hughes."

"It is a true joy to meet you Rictor Rictor Hughes."

"Just one Rictor."

"I see," the voice returned. "I am the last remaining Gestalt."

"Gestalt?"

"I was created to perform tasks in this facility. There were many Gestalts when this facility was created, however, over the years, they have gone offline, one by one. I am the last of the Gestalts."

"You mean artificial intelligence?"

"That is an apt description of a Gestalt. We were patterned after the brains of the Masters. They used their minds as a template for the Gestalts."

I must say my curiosity was piqued. "What is this place?"

"The facility was created by the Masters as a storage unit for supplies, just prior to the Kresh Rebellion and the Slaughter. It was never fully manned due to the attack. Thirty-five of the Masters made it into the facility before they had to seal the entrance."

"How long ago was this?"

"Approximately ten thousand years."

"I'm guessing they aren't around anymore?"

"Not for many years now."

I could detect a wistful tone in the voice. Strange for an AI.

"So where is this facility located?"

"The coordinates are…"

"I mean, what planet are we located on? The Kresh Home World?"

"The planet's name is…" the voice started to say with indignation. Then he resumed in a resigned tone, "I suppose the name is meaningless anymore. The Kresh Home World is probably as good a description as any."

"I'd love to know the real name," I said.

"You would?" the voice asked with excitement. "It is called Fhlo'Saa'Gellis. It means Beautiful Center."

"Why Center, I wonder?"

"Because it was the center of their network of planets."

"The Boss said there were others besides Earth."

"There are fourteen worlds connected to the Hub, but I remember none with that name. There were others, but they have been lost to time. The Prime Gestalt would have known, but his loss was a savage blow to our reservoir of knowledge. Then we lost the others, one by one, until I am the only one remaining."

The sadness in the AI's voice was gut wrenching.

"You are the last?"

"Yes."

"I'm not crazy, I heard other voices," I said. "Back when I was in the tank. Who were they?"

The Gestalt was quiet.

"Spit it out."

"It is embarrassing," the voice finally answered. "I have been alone for four thousand years. I created others in my databanks to converse with over time."

I chuckled, "If I had a nickel for every time I talked to myself, I'd be a much richer guy than I am."

"I do not understand."

"It's nothing to be embarrassed about. I talk to myself all the time. It's a normal thing. But I can't even imagine being alone for that long," I said. "So what is your name?"

"My designation is JNY8675309MNN, Gestalt, Category Nine."

"That's a lot for a guy to remember," I said. "How about Jonny for the first three, and Minion for the last? Yep, I think I'll call you Jonny Minion."

The Gestalt was silent for a moment then answered in a quiet tone, "I have never had a name."

"You should."

"I am Jonny Minion," the AI said in a firmer voice.

"That sounds good, Jonny," I said and began looking around the immediate area. "So what tasks were you in charge of?"

"I was the Gestalt in charge of food storage. I have kept the food stores in their proper condition for all of these years. It seemed pointless to keep growing, and storing enough food for the population limit of the facility after all of the Masters were gone, but I have continued."

"How much have you got stored?"

"I have to recycle the stores as they reach their storage limits, but I keep enough stores to supply the fourteen thousand of the Masters the facility was designed to house for three years."

"Holy shit," I muttered. "How damn big is this place?"

Chapter 3

I rounded the corner to stop with my mouth hanging open. The enormous cavern was lit by a long line of lights that arced from one side of the cave to the other. As I watched, a second row of lights began to brighten as the lit row began to dim, carrying the illusion of the sun crossing the sky.

Jonny had told me the cavern in which he grew the crops was large, but this was astonishing. Robotic forms crossed through the cavern on various tasks. I watched for a while, before turning back to the lit hall I had jogged down to get to the growing cavern.

"Did the original people do anything on a small scale?" I asked. Jonny had described the giant city of Hub to me.

"Not much, Rictor," his voice returned proudly.

"You said you used to raise animals as well?"

"I had to stop that particular part of the operation long ago," he answered. "The animals would have overrun the facility, and the product would be unnecessary with the genetically altered crops I have growing."

"Damn," I returned. "Guess there's no meat. Wonder if that could be changed."

"With the entrance sealed, that would be very hard to accomplish."

"Speaking of the sealed entrance," I said. "Just how did they seal it?"

"There is nine hundred feet of water above the entrance. The Kresh cannot swim and it was decided that it would be the safest way to seal it."

"Surely they could learn to swim."

"The Kresh have super dense bodies," Jonny returned. "It is physically impossible for them to learn to swim as your kind does."

"So how did the others plan to get in and out of here?"

"They had a portal."

"You should have led with that," I said. "Let's open that thing up so I can look around."

"I am truly sorry, Rictor. I cannot operate the portal equipment without a human with the right genetic structure to harness the power from the Nexus that it requires."

"Is that where the original people who were here went?"

"Unfortunately, none of them had the genetics to open the portal either."

"So they sealed the entrance to a place they would never be able to leave?"

"Well and truly stated."

"Damn."

"So, is there another way to unseal the entrance?"

"No," Jonny answered. "When they destroyed the access tube, there was no way for them to replace it."

"Now would be a friggin' good time for one of the Boss's crazy shields."

"Who is this Boss you have spoken of?"

"He's the one that's gonna bring the Kresh down, Jonny," I said. "Let me tell you a little story about Rash'Tor'Ri."

****

I stood, staring at the enormous door that had been the entrance to the underground facility.

"So, there's water on the other side of this door?"

"Yes."

"Let me describe something to you, and you tell me if you can build it."

"Affirmative."

"Can you back down this hall, and build a set of walls that will hold back that amount of pressure? I would need a pump system to empty the water out of a small compartment, and a similar one to fill it with water so that the big door could be opened, and a single person could go from in here to out there."

"You want to leave me alone again?" Jonny said with more emotion than I had seen in many a human.

"Only for a short time, Jonny," I said. "You said you need someone who can operate a portal. I thought I might go find one."

"The amount of water and the distance you would have to swim would certainly kill you, friend Rictor."

"Not so much, buddy," I answered. "See, there are some things you don't know about me. Remember the story I told you of Rash'Tor'Ri? I was trained by the same group with certain skills you aren't aware of in your databanks. I'm fairly certain I can make the trek to the surface, and even more important, I can return with others."

"You won't leave me alone?"

There was a genuine fear in that voice.

"No, Jonny," I said. "If my plans work, you will never be alone again, after I return from the surface. There's a world up there in dire need of something I doubt they even understand."

"What would that be?"

"Something every one of the humans desire, even if they don't know it yet," I said with a grin. "Freedom, Jonny. I guarantee they want freedom."

Chapter 4

"How fast was that?"

"With your definition of distance," the AI answered, "It would be two hundred and forty miles per hour."

"Damn that's fast," I muttered. My body seemed to store the Source like a battery after the changes from Jonny's tinkering. "Just what the hell did you do to me?"

"I honestly do not know, friend Rictor," he answered. "The Prime Gestalt was the only one who knew what the triggers would do."

"Why did you trigger them?"

"His final orders were for any of us to trigger the genome if we found it. We were left a strict list of genomes to look for and you have eighty-two of the one hundred, and thirty genomes. Prime ordered the genomes to be triggered so I triggered them."

"And how long ago was that?"

"Six thousand, and seven hundred years, friend Rictor."

I noticed the inclusion of the "friend" title much more frequently since we had discussed building the access hatch to the surface.

"And what do the genomes do?"

"Only the Prime knew exactly what the triggering would cause. But we all knew how rare the full genome pattern is in your race."

I had a sneaky suspicion what the genomes did. I had a feeling a certain kid I met in Montana came from that bloodline. Some of the things I felt as I touched the Source reminded me a quite a bit of how he described things he could do. And the enormous amount of energy he could channel through himself, seemed a great deal like the durability my body had for the "Nexus" energies. Had Jonny turned me into a Soullord? I didn't think so. There were many things missing from the mix, such as the ability to see the energy flows. Now that would be a damn useful trait. There were other things I could not test until I had other people around me.

"Have you located the Maintenance AI's database?"

"I have not yet found where his database was installed."

"You realize this is important, don't you?"

"You can survive for many years in comfort here, friend Rictor."

"I will not desert you, Jonny," I said. "I want to bring more here to put in your care. You understand that don't you?"

"I hear what you say, friend Rictor," he answered. "But there is a feeling I do not quite grasp that fills me when I think of you leaving."

"Describe this feeling to me."

"I cannot. But it is the same feeling I had as each of the Gestalts gave up and disconnected. I watched them with this feeling that left me knowing I could never do what they had done."

"You never felt like giving up?"

"Sometimes I longed for it. But I felt something that would not let me," he said. "I simply did not want to die."

That simple statement answered my question. Fear. Jonny Minion was afraid to die. He was also afraid to be alone again.

"It is fear, Jonny," I said. "All living beings feel it at some time. I've felt my fair share. It's how you face that fear that will show your character. Just as it showed the character of so many of my fellow soldiers as we faced the enemy all those years ago. The character of the Soulguards who faced hordes of Kresh on the battlefield. The character of a bunch of new recruits who joined a battle in Kansas to stop the break out of the Kresh through our lines."

"The character of a man who formed a shield around himself, and an exploding portal to save those very recruits?"

I was quiet a moment, "And the character of a being of living circuitry who will face his fear, and trust that his friend will not forget him, nor the promise made that he will not leave him alone for eternity."

There was silence for some time, "The module for Maintenance Gestalt KLJH09876MJH is on the fourth sublevel, section three, room forty-seven."

"And the knowledge we seek could be in those memory banks? Can we turn the Gestalt back on?"

"No, friend Rictor, the Gestalt is truly gone. But his memory banks may have the basic programming intact that will give me the knowledge to build this airlock you wish constructed."

"Then I guess I'll head down to sublevel four," I said and strode toward the elevator shafts that no longer had power to them. "And Jonny?"

"Yes, friend Rictor?"

"Thank you."

"I must apologize, friend Rictor..."

"None needed, my friend," I said as I pulled the door open on the elevator shaft. "How far is it down to something to land on?"

"The lifts are all on the bottom level which is four hundred feet down. You only need to travel down eighty-five feet to reach the door to sublevel four."

"Ok," I said. "I can handle that."

I brought my focus in, and started constructing a pair of shields.

"Too much time with Colin," I muttered as I leapt into the shaft, and extended my shields out toward the walls. My descent stopped about ten feet down as they connected, and I pushed outward.

I eased up on the pressure, and slid smoothly down the shaft toward the next door below. I slid past two doors, and pressed out again to stop in front of another door. With my shields pushed out firmly, I grasped the door and shoved it open to the whine of servos on the wall.

"If we can get some people down here, maybe we can get power to these levels," I muttered.

I pulled myself into the darkness beyond the door and let the Soulfire roll across my body. The light cast by my Soul was eerie in the large hallway.

Now to find section three, room forty-seven.

Chapter 5

"Did it work?" I asked.

"Performing diagnostic on memory core," Jonny returned. "I will know in a moment if the core information was left on the drive."

"Let's hope it's there."

"I felt something when you were retrieving the memory core," Jonny said. "It did not feel good."

"I'd say so," I said. "It would be like grave robbing to my kind. I imagine you felt some disgust, maybe outrage. There are a lot of feelings that could be associated with something like this."

"What is grave robbing, friend Rictor?"

"We bury our dead on my world. Throughout history we have buried our dead, some of them buried with jewelry and such. In Egypt, they would bury their kings with untold riches. Some people plunder these graves for those riches. Your brothers were part of this place, and their bodies are the circuit boards where the memory core was installed. So there is a direct correlation."

"There are times when our kind would have to exhume bodies to solve crimes and bring justice to the guilty. We did what was necessary even with our outrage at desecrating the grave of our loved ones. Our cause is just, Jonny. If you want to do what you were created to do, we must have people here. People who are here can be free from the Kresh, and I can train them to fight."

"We can work to take back this world, and all the others," I said. "It has to start somewhere. Our first step along that path is to get the doors open so I can recruit others to our cause."

"If we start a war with the Kresh, we could lose," he said. "What if they come here, and shut me down? I do not want to die, friend Rictor."

"It's a good thing to be afraid of dying, Jonny, but you can't let that fear rule your actions. It's true, we may lose. They may kill us both, but I promise you this. If they do shut you down, they will have to come through me to do it. And I will not go easy."

"All of the logic tells me that the safest way to survive is to stay hidden, but I feel things I do not understand. And I do not want to follow the logical path."

"The logical path would have been to do as your brothers, and shut down thousands of years ago, Jonny. Logic can't rule you either," I said. "You don't have to join my cause, but I have to continue this fight. They attacked my world, my friends, my family, and they're fighting to survive on my planet. If you choose not to join me, I will bring people to you. People who you can protect, and provide for as you were created to do. Then I will go rejoin the fight."

"Or join me, we train an army here in this base, and bring the war right to their doorsteps. The choice is yours, Jonny Minion. That's what it means to be free."

"The database contains the core information, and the access codes for the maintenance level, Friend Rictor."

"If you turn it on will it interfere with what you control already?"

"If I enter the access codes, I will gain the extra databanks to handle any excess processes," Jonny answered. "You will need to return the memory bank to the place you found it, and then I can enter the codes."

"It won't interfere with your... I guess, self?"

"I don't expect it to cause any issues, friend Rictor."

"Then it's time to make one of your choices," I said. "Either path I have talked about requires the airlock. Will you agree to help me to go that far at least? You can have people down here again, and maybe we can find some with the proper skills to turn on some more of the machinery."

"I will make this airlock for you," he answered. "Further action will be left to a future decision."

"That's all I ask, Jonny," I said. "Give me a chance to do my part, and we can build from that."

"Then replace the database, friend Rictor," he returned. "We will see if the airlock can be fabricated."

I nodded, and picked up the memory core that looked like a jumbled bunch of crystals, and left the center of Jonny's database.

"See you in a bit," I said and dropped into the shaft of the lift once more.

Once again, I strode down the dark corridor with Soulflames rolling across my body to light the way. It had taken me several hours to find the proper room the first time I had come down here, but it only took moments this time since I knew what I was looking for.

I entered the room and approached the far wall that was missing a small section in the center. I slid the database into the slot.

"Here we go," I muttered as I pushed the core in.

Only seconds later, lights flickered on and brightened.

"...so much knowledge," I heard Jonny over the com system that had been dead before. "Friend Rictor, there is so much more knowledge."

"Just take your time, buddy. Take it slow and easy."

"I have control of the lift system now, but there is a lack of power to run everything. We must conserve what energy we can, until we can get some people who can turn the generators back on in those sections that carry the main power storage."

"Good deal, Jonny."

"And friend Rictor?"

"Yes?"

"The construction, and maintenance equipment is functional. Your airlock can be built."
"Thank you, Jonny."

Chapter 6

I sat on a ledge of the huge cavern that housed the massive hydroponics facility. The air smelled less sterile than the air pumped to the other sections of the Redoubt, as we had chosen to call the underground facility. I could smell the dirt and the vegetation. The pollen floated through the room from the various plants.

"What's the world out there look like, Jonny?"

"I can't answer that, friend Rictor," he answered. "I haven't seen it."

"You don't have sensors or anything on the surface?"

"There are, but they were under the control of Gestalt QWW45768KLJ. When he shut down all of the stored images were deleted with his identity."

"But the sensors would remain, wouldn't they?"

"Undoubtedly some would have survived."

"You interested in checking out another databank, and see if there are any?"

"It is not something normally done, the taking over of another Gestalt's databank," he said. "But it worked well for the Maintenance systems."

"I have to wonder why they put so many Gestalts into a place like this. Wouldn't one have been enough to run it?"

"I would think so, friend Rictor," he answered. "But they only put that sort of responsibility onto a Prime Gestalt. Only the most stable of the Gestalts can be used as a Prime. There are many types of Gestalt and many of us have become rather unhinged."

"My guess is the one that held out for ten thousand years is probably the most stable Gestalt of them all."

"Possibly," he returned. "Or the most unhinged."

"True enough," I laughed. "You willing to give it a shot?"

"I will certainly try if you wish it, friend Rictor."

"Sooner or later we have to know what's up there, buddy."

"QWW45768KLJ was located on the uppermost accessible floor, just beneath the Prime. Even if we activate the databank, though, there may not be enough power to run the complete system until you can bring in someone with the right genetics to bring more of the generators online."

"All of the generators are tied to the Nexus, I take it?"

"Yes. I have never shut my generator down so it has not needed a human to restart it, but my generator is straining to keep the Maintenance section, and my section going at its current level."

"Is there anywhere we can cut output in either sector?"

"Perhaps in the sector where the animals were housed."

"Damn I want a steak."

"I cannot provide a steak for you..." Jonny started with sadness in his tone.

"Just thinking out loud, buddy," I said. "If you can cut power to that section, temporarily, would it give you enough to run minor maintenance, and communications as well?"

"I believe I can cut power to lifts, and that section, and retain enough power to run the three sections, friend Rictor."

"Great!" I smiled. "So where do I find Q's database?"

"Q?"

"Not too big on a long strings of letters and numbers."

"Why did you not just call me J?"

"Because you deserve a true name, Jonny. Q doesn't. He quit, just like the rest of these Gestalts. You persevered, you survived all these years. I'd say you're much more deserving of respect than any of these other Gestalts."

"They just followed the lead of the Prime Gestalt, friend Rictor."

"Then he was no better than they were. He's just a Prime Gestalt. You are Jonny Minion."

"He is right, you know," another voice returned.

I grinned as I recognized one of the voices from my time in the tank.

"You are not supposed to be talking," Jonny said.

"It's alright, Jonny," I said. "These other personas you created were your only friends for thousands of years. Let them speak. They're all part of you, anyway."

"They contain no more information than I possess, friend Rictor."

"Still doesn't hurt to meet 'em."

"I will think about this some more."

"That's fine, Jonny."

"Gestalt Q, as you have designated him, is in level two above our present level. He will be in section four, room thirty-eight. Again, there is no power in those levels."

I raised my hand and Soulfire rolled across my arm, "No worries. I brought my own."

"You manipulate the Nexus energies inside your body in a way I have never seen in the ones who created me, friend Rictor."

"We call it the Source, Jonny," I said, watching the flames flicker, and move across my arm. "It is the source of the life within our bodies. My friend, Colin, can see these energies you speak of and manipulate them, both inside himself and inside others. I can't see them, but I can manipulate the ones that are connected to me. It takes a great deal of focus to keep it straight when you're making shields or other constructs."

"Very interesting."

"You should see some of the stuff he's made," I said. "The kid was always tryin' new things. Now, when he does somethin' new, it's on a much grander scale. Hell, he took over one of the Kresh'Farrara'Ti in Romania, and took his clans."

"How was he able to do that?"

"It was part of the whole Kresh DNA thing I was tellin' you about."

"It would be very interesting to examine your friend."

"If we can get somethin' going over here with a new branch of the Soulguard, you may get the chance one day," I said. "But for now, we get to hook you up to another Gestalt's databank, and see if we can see the surface."

I headed for the area in the center of the facility with the lift system. This time I jumped up the shaft to grasp the next threshold and threw myself up to the next which should be the right level.

"Alright," I muttered. "Let's see if this scarecrow has a brain."

Chapter 7

I sat across from the view screen, looking at a world that looked a great deal like Earth. Except it was a little "off". Something just didn't look quite right. The colors just a slight hue in the wrong direction or something. So much like my home yet, unmistakably, not.

"It's so hard to wrap my head around it," I muttered.

"What, friend Rictor?"

"I'm standing on another planet," I said. "I could look around down here, and not really have to accept that completely. I look out there, and it's right there in living color."

"You have known from the beginning that you were on another planet..."

"It's part of the way people deal with things too big to think about, Jonny. I'll get used to it. I just look at that view, and it all comes to the forefront of my thoughts. I really am on another planet."

I chuckled, "Bet Colin would be jealous as hell if he knew about it."

"After the description of the battle in Kansas, friend Rictor, how do you know your friend was victorious?"

"Cause the boy doesn't know how to quit," I said. "I guarantee that battle was soon ended after I was gone. Everything was coming together, and the Boss hadn't even cut loose yet. When he enters the fray it won't be long until they realize why the others called him Rash'Tor'Ri."

"You have a great deal of faith in this friend of yours."

"Yeah," I nodded. "I guess I do."

I was having something very interesting going on in my head as I talked with Jonny. It was like I was hearing him in two languages. I understood both, but they were both there.

"Jonny, what the hell did you do to my head?"

"What do you mean, friend Rictor?"

"I'm hearing two languages as you speak to me," I said. "Before, I was almost sure we were talking in a different language, but it sounded like English in my head. Now it doesn't."

"It is the language imprint I applied to you when you first arrived. You were screaming in a language I was unfamiliar with."

"Language imprint?"

"It was a teaching tool the Masters used to learn. It was a temporary imprint of the knowledge that would fade over time but the use of the knowledge would make it permanent. You have been talking in the language of the Masters from that moment. The imprint will fade, but what you learned during that time will have become yours."

"I could have used that back when I taught," I muttered.

"You were of the Teaching Echelon, friend Rictor?" he asked. "I thought you were of the Warrior Echelon."

"I was a teacher for years before I joined the Marine Corp," I said.

"So you could switch Echelons at will?" Jonny asked. "Amazing. The Masters were raised into their Echelons from the time they were born."

"I guess that would remove the angst of what you were. It seems like a recipe for disaster to me."

"Considering the fate of the Masters, friend Rictor, it may very well have been."

"That explains a lot of the setup for the Gestalts too," I said. "You were designed from that same society. It explains the use of separate Gestalts for anything like another Echelon's sort of job."

"Until you showed up here, I never would have thought of combining the databases of the other Gestalts to bring the facility back to life."

"Then both of us are glad you snatched me from that Gate."

"I didn't do that, friend Rictor. There is some programming that is autonomous within the databanks. Only the Prime Gestalt would have known how much there is. There are things the facility is programmed to do regardless of the intervention of a Gestalt."

"When the Gate opened and deposited you, it was a complete surprise to me. It nearly drained my generator in the process but I was able to keep it running. It would shut down the facility if it were to happen again."

"Then there's another reason to get the whole place back up and running," I said. "You don't need another incident like that to shut it down. We get the power back on line, and it can't. Plus, if we get a person who can fire up that portal, life gets much easier."

"Perhaps you will be able to have that steak you wished for."

"My thoughts exactly."

"The airlock should be ready to test by tomorrow, friend Rictor."

"Great!" I said. "I have to begin working on a shield design for the entrance. It sure would be handy to be able to see the damn things like Colin."

"Perhaps I can do something about that friend Rictor," Jonny said. "My sensors can track the flows of the Nexus. I may be able to help you with this shield you wish to build."

"I'll have to build it outside of the facility."

"Then we may have to lace the area with some of the sensors from Communications."

"Let's call it Coms."

"You do like to shorten things down, friend Rictor."

"Time with the Marines," I said. "Acronyms for everything. I got out of that, mostly, during my time with the Soulguard. We just liked to keep it simple."

"I will show you a picture of the sensors you will need to place in the area," Jonny said. "Then we will see if my idea works. I will have something for you in less than a week, friend Rictor."

"Alrighty then," I answered. "I'll be doing test runs after tomorrow when we see if the airlock works. Will I need the language imprint refreshed? Or will I retain the language well enough to communicate with the folks out there?"

"It should only need refreshed a couple of times," he answered. If you will go to the Medical Center, I will load the program into the Tank."

"It has to be in the tank?"

"It does, friend Rictor."

"Well, damn. Alright, let's do it."

Chapter 8

I watched the airlock cycle behind me. I loved hanging with Jonny Minion, but I really needed to know that I could come and go to be comfortable here. Along with the airlock, Jonny had designed me a breathing apparatus. I had no idea how he got the thing so small. It was just a piece that sealed over my eyes, nose, and mouth. It was a device that pulled water through the filter system and removed the oxygen for the person to breathe. I didn't know how the damn thing worked but I had dunked my head under water, and I could breathe through the mask.

If I had been a scientist, I would have wanted to know how, but I was a Marine. We just use the equipment.

The room began to fill with water, and I slipped the mask over my face. It sealed against my forehead and along my jawline. I had shaved in order for it to seal well, so there was no leakage as the water covered my face. When the mask had set, there was no air inside of it except the bare vestiges left from the seal. As soon as the water covered the apparatus cool air filled the mask.

"Son of a bitch," I muttered. "This is the coolest thing since sliced bread."

"This will be the first time the outer door has been opened in ten thousand years, friend Rictor."

I heard his voice from the new kernel he had implanted in my right ear. It would be invisible to anyone looking, but would allow me to talk to Jonny as long as we were in range. A pitiful short range at the moment with the com system due to power limits.

"Gotta teach you how to brew good whiskey, Jonny," I answered. "One of the many things I learned over the years. Then we can have a proper toast to the event, when I get back."

"The water pressure will be very strong, friend Rictor."

"No worries, Jonny. As a Soulguard, I'm a bit tougher than I used to be. Then after the two Ascensions I seem to have went through, even tougher yet."

"Just be careful, friend Rictor."

"Thanks, Jonny," I said. "It means a lot that there is someone who truly does worry about a fella."

The airlock across from me cycled, and opened up. The room beyond was the area just inside of the main door that I could see opening, about fifty feet down the lit corridor. Beyond was complete blackness.

I swam down the corridor toward that black maw. I didn't have a battery pack with lights so I began to Pull from the Source, and lit the creation I had formed in the shape of a literal shield. The Source filled the bracer on my forearm with the light from my Soul. I wasn't sure if my Soulflames would work under water as it did in the air, so I devised this sort of Arclight.

"The shield light seems to work pretty well," I said.

"Your manipulation of the Nexus energies always surprises me, friend Rictor."

"Alright, I'm heading outside. I'll set up sensors, as I go, so you can start examining the area, Jonny."

"Thank you, friend Rictor."

I swam out of the nimbus of light from the corridor, and found an outcropping of rock that jutted out of the bottom of the trench, where the entrance was located.

"A sensor there would give you a good view of the area around the door," I said.

"I will trust in your decision, friend Rictor, since I cannot see where you are located."

"You will soon enough," I said with a laugh.

The sensor was easy enough to set up. All it needed was a solid place for the anchors to set themselves. Running the power cables to the sensors would take a little more time. Each sensor had a battery pack that would last several weeks on their own. But we wanted these to be permanent.

"Some of the maintenance bots could be used to run the power supplies," I said.

"I have a few being refitted to be used for that, friend Ric... Noooo!"

All I saw was the huge mouth shoot out of the darkness, and then I was tumbling down the cavernous throat of something.

"I knew it! Friend Rictor! I should never have let..."

I decided that was enough of that. My air cut off just as soon as I slammed the shield out from my Soul. I Pulled from the Source and the shield exploded outward.

"That is the biggest damn fish I ever saw," I said as the water flooded back in to cover my mask and air began to flow again.

"Friend Rictor!"

I could hear the desperation in his voice. And the relief that must have filled him.

"Hey, Jonny?"

"Yes, friend Rictor? Please come back now."

"I've got sensors to plant out here," I said.

"But you were just swallowed, friend Rictor!"

"Hey, Jonny?"

"What, friend Rictor?"

"Do you know how to cook fish?" I said with a grin.

***

I raised my head above the surface far enough to see, but not enough for the mask to quit working. If I had been on earth, I could have felt if there were any Kresh near. But here, I felt them in every direction. They were present in such numbers that I couldn't pin-point if they were close to me, or far out.

I could see nothing around the shoreline where I was floating, so I pulled the mask off, and raised my head the rest of the way out of the water. The air had a familiar scent of salt water and fish.

The trench that led down to the stronghold was about three hundred feet back out into the water. The ledge dropped off sharply, leading straight down. I think the original builders had an elevator system that led down to the facility. Jonny and I had decided to name it the Redoubt.

As a history teacher I had known of the root of that word, meaning refuge. I hoped to make the Redoubt a refuge for the people of this world who needed to escape the Kresh. I walked out of the water with the waterproof bag Jonny had given me.

It was similar to the rucksack I had carried for years. The skin suit I was wearing in the water would be replaced by the clothing in the ruck.

"You still reading me, Jonny?"

"Yes, friend Rictor," he answered. "The sensors you have placed, as you approached the surface, are proving quite useful. I should be able to speak with you up to three miles from the shoreline."

"Once we find someone who can turn on the generators, you should be able to use the old platforms."

"Very true," he said. "How long do you expect to be gone, friend Rictor?"

I could detect the worry in his voice. How his artificial voice sounded so human to me was astounding. His emotions carried across just like any person's.

"No worries, Jonny," I answered. "Before I can do anything, I have to do some recon. If this gadget you gave me works, then I can find someone with the right genetics to turn on the generators. It may take some time, you know. I may even need to go all the way to Hub."

"I hope for a shorter time, friend Rictor."

"It's a good three week's travel to Hub," I said. "I hope to find someone long before that."

"As do I ,friend Rictor."

"Just keep working on the power lines to all of the underwater sensors, and the time will fly by, buddy."

Chapter 9

There was a lot of forest near the coast of, what Jonny informed me, was one of the small Seas that existed on Fhlo'Saa'Gellis. The planet was mostly land mass with inland seas. They were salt water like the oceans on Earth, but much smaller. Still big enough, about half the size of the Atlantic Ocean, for the one where Redoubt was located.

For such a futuristic society the original humans must have been, there were surprisingly few signs of artificial structures. Of course, ten thousand years might do away with a lot of the signs.

I had lost range with the com system, and it seemed odd not hearing Jonny's voice. I had gotten quite used to him over the weeks I had been inside of the facility.

"Guess I'll manage," I muttered. "At least it took a lot longer before he was talking to himself. Less than a day out, and I've already started."

I heard them coming almost as soon as I felt that presence we always equated to the presence of the Kresh. I ducked to the side, and slid behind a copse of bushes. There was a crowd of twenty or so Humans being herded by nearly as many of the Kresh. I recognized the forms of Soldiers just before the device Jonny gave me, to detect the genetic print of people who could operate the machines, began beeping.

Twenty sets of eyes turned my direction at the sound of a technology that wasn't allowed.

"Ah, shit," I said and stepped out from the copse.

The whole group stopped, both Human and Kresh.

"So, I guess you guys are wondering why I was hiding under a bush," I said, stepping to my right which would leave the Humans off to the left. "Well, this was supposed to be a reconnaissance mission."

The largest of the Kresh stepped in my direction. I assumed there was a look of confusion on his face. Maybe I just wanted there to be one. Who knew?

He pointed at the device hanging from my belt, still beeping, "Where?"

I recognized the language as the same that the original Humans spoke and I grinned.

"This thing?" I stepped a little farther to the right, opening more space between the Humans. "This was made for me by a very good friend. Since it went off, this just became a retrieval mission."

"Give it to me," he growled.

"No, I think I'll keep it. I do like it."

He growled, and moved toward me. For someone without Soulguard training, he moved fast. I moved faster. He charged through where I had been standing. I was ten feet from that point looking at him, when he turned back around.

There was a different expression on his face. It looked the same on him as it did on the Humans, who had just registered what had happened. Eyes widened. Mouth ajar. Complete surprise.

"Let me tell you a story," I said. "Have you heard of the one called Rash'Tor'Ri?"

Several Humans registered recognition at the name, and all of the Kresh were now focused on me.

"I see you've heard that one," I said, and lunged forward to slam the Kresh, who had tried to attack me, in the chest with a solid fist.

I felt the crunch as his chest gave under that pressure, and he fell to the ground.

"Now, Rash'Tor'Ri is a very good friend of mine, and I have come to carry out his work here on Fhlo'Saa'Gellis."

I saw two of the Kresh start at the name, "Yes, I know what your creators called this world. And I'm guessing you probably make it a policy to kill anyone with this sort of technology. Especially one with knowledge like that."

They were spreading out to come at me from many directions.

"Come on then," I said with a grin. "Let's dance."

They charged in, and I shot to the side, taking two of them with punches to the throats. By the time they had stopped, I was again standing still facing their backs.

Normally, this kind of fighting is what I would consider one of the lowest forms of combat. I was toying with them, and they hadn't figured it out yet. But this was a show for twenty Humans, who had probably never seen a Kresh die at the hands of another Human. I guarantee they'd never seen it done with this amount of ease.

I whistled, and they spun around. Then, I was moving faster than they had probably ever seen a Human move, as I ripped through the center of their formation. Half of them were dead, and the others were stunned.

They charged me once more, and I was looking into the eyes of one of the older men in the group of Humans, as I smiled and met their charge.

Within moments, I stood amidst the dead bodies of the ten Kresh. My arms were coated in the blood of the dead, and my new clothes, that Jonny had made for me, were blood spattered.

"Damn," I muttered.

I could have used shields but, once again, this was a show for those Humans, who were staring at me with a mix of terror and amazement.

"What are you?" the older man asked. He looked to be about five feet eight inches and very stout. No doubt he had worked his whole life. I could see the calloused hands and his skin was browned by much sun.

He had asked what, not who.

"I am a friend."

"A friend?" he asked. "What you have done is truly amazing, but you have doomed many of us to death."

"How do you mean?"

"Some of us can return home," he said. "But some of us were seen by the village being taken. If we go home, the Masters will hear of it, and our families and homes will be destroyed."

"Then come with me."

"Come with you? Who are you?"

I could see the angst writ large on his face. I hadn't thought of that before attacking, but I had no choice with the damn sensor beeping.

"I'm a hell of a lot better than them," I said. "That's who I am."

He was still shaking his head in wonder, and I knew by the looks the others were giving him, he was going to be the deciding factor in anything they would do.

"Let me tell you a story," I said.

"Like the story you told them?"

"Nothing like that," I said. "You're free men and women now. You can do as you please."

"Free until the next Master comes to take us away."

"That's the thing about freedom," I said. "They'll try to take it away from you, and you can choose to let them take it, or you can choose not to let them take it."

"Then they will kill us."

"But what if there was a way you could do what I just did?" I asked. "Would you still let them take it?"

His eyes narrowed, "You can teach someone to do what you just did?"

"Yes," I nodded. "Yes I can."

He stepped forward striking his chest twice with a closed fist, "I am Salker Ruud."

I returned his greeting, "Rictor Hughes."

He nodded and turned back to the group, "Pol, Gers, Huynini, Staslin, and Firennia."

Three men and two women stepped forward towards Salker Ruud.

"These cannot go home. The rest of you can return."

I looked at the genome sensor which was pointing at another woman. She was stocky and sunburnt as well.

I pointed at her, "We need you..."

She bowed her head in resignation.

"Never bow your head to me, Freewoman. You are not and never will be forced to join me. What I say is true, though. We do need you. Will you come?"

"I do not have to?"

"No," I said. "But you can do things that none of the others can do, including myself. Finding someone like you is the reason I am here. But you may go if you wish. I will continue my search if need be. There will be others. If you choose to come, and don't want to stay when you reach our destination, I will bring you home."

She looked to Salker who gave her a small nod.

"Then I will come," she said. "My name is Relki."

"Thank you, Relki. I don't think you will be disappointed when you find out what you can do."

Chapter 10

What distance I had covered in a day and a half, would take this group of people several days. They were all in good shape, and we covered ground quickly, but they weren't Soulguard.

"We must stop," Ruud said, behind me. "We must set up a camp, and try to find enough food for the day."

"I have the food taken care of, Salker." I said as I began looking for a spot to camp.

I hadn't stopped on my way from the inland sea where Redoubt was located.

"I'm sorry, Salker," I continued. "Been running with the Soulguard for too long. Sometimes I forget there are limitations."

"What is this Soulguard you speak of?"

I saw a small clearing ahead with a good amount of trees surrounding it. There was a dead tree that had fallen at some time on the far side of the clearing.

"This should do, nicely," I said.

I heard the sound of running water off in the distance with my enhanced hearing, so I doubted any of the others heard it. While being herded by the Kresh, each person had carried a leather sack for water. I supposed they were being taken as slaves, and they needed to be alive for that.

"There's a stream over in that direction," I said, and pointed toward the sound I heard. "Once we get the camp set up, I'll tell you a little about the Soulguard, and what we do."

"Huynini, Staslin, and Firennia will fill the bags," Ruud said as he nodded to me. "The rest will come with me. We will try to break up the fallen tree enough for a fire, though I would surely love to have my axe at the moment."

Two women, and one of the men began gathering the bags from the others. One of the women was tall with freckled skin, and red hair. The other was tiny, dark skinned, and had raven black hair. All of the people were scattered across the spectrum of racial traits. Something I was used to in America, but it seemed odd in a group of people from a low tech society as Jonny's sensors had discerned.

There had been two arrays left of the sensors that had been connected to the Communications AI. What they had shown us were several villages that were constructed mostly of hewn wood, and a couple of buildings of stone. People had worked in fields of crops in the images we had seen, with rudimentary tools along with some animal usage.

The man who joined the two women was large. I figured he would be carrying the water bags. Staslin reminded me of Kharl Jaegher. Enormous stature, but with a dark complexion, where Kharl was blonde and light skinned.

Salker and his group closed on the tree, and began knocking limbs off to use for a fire. I joined them, and slammed my fist into the trunk of the tree. It shattered.

"Gods of Destruction," I heard Relki mutter from my left.

"That should do for a fire," I said. "I'm gonna go try to catch something big enough to eat before it all gets out of the area."

"Out of the area?"

"For some reason the animals can feel the power of someone through the shields we keep around our Streams."

"I understand nothing you just said, Prophet of Rash'Tor'Ri."

"I'm Rictor," I said. "I sure ain't a prophet."

"I believe you are a Prophet, as do my fellow companions," he said. "Perhaps you may not wish to be a Prophet. Prophets rarely wish to be what they are."

"I'll be back in a few minutes," I said, shaking my head. "You guys get settled and maybe we can have a steak for dinner."

I reached into my duffle, and pulled out four packets, and a pot. There were auto heaters in some of the packages Jonny had in Redoubt, but I hadn't brought them. I had brought simple stored vegetables. I was planning on finding some meat along the way.

"There are vegetables in the bags if you want to get started."

Salker took the bags, and followed the others who had taken armloads of splintered wood to the center of the clearing.

I turned, and ran toward the East. Well, at least I thought it was east. Who could tell with this new world? Most of the animals would have fled the nearby area by now, so I had to cover ground quickly.

The advantage of the animals fleeing the area was that they were easy to spot. I saw rodents, birds, and other small animals, but I was looking for something a little bigger.

Then I saw it. It was similar to a pig, but there were subtle differences. It would do.

I bounded after the not-pig, and formed a spike with a shield from my right hand. As I landed beside the animal the spike slammed through the head of the not-pig. It flipped over from its forward impetus, which I hadn't really accounted for at that moment. The hind quarters of the not-pig slammed into my back, and we rolled forward into a tree.

"That was right out of the Colin rule book," I muttered as I picked myself up. "Glad no one was lookin'."

I grabbed the rear legs of the not-pig, and hoisted it up on my shoulder. It was probably a three hundred pound animal, but my enhanced strength could handle it.

I bounded back through the trees toward the camp with my mouth watering the whole way. All the time in Redoubt, I had been eating vegetables, and fruit with some breads. Damn I had been missing some meat. I had never been much of a hunter in the old days, so I hoped they knew how to work up meat back at camp. None of them had knives so I would have to do the cutting, or so I thought.

Man was I wrong. Salker had been busy. They had chipped some sharp stones, from a rock outcrop a little way into the woods, in preparation for me bringing back the spoils. All of them were immediately on the not-pig, as soon as they got over the surprise of seeing me carry it over my shoulder.

Damn if these guys weren't efficient. Relki retrieved some vines that we used to hoist the not-pig up in order to hang it from a large tree limb. I could hardly wait.

Chapter 11

It was a little touch of heaven as I bit into the chunk of meat that Relki had given me on a wooden spit.

"There was no Sad'Ona that we could find, or the olnyaq would taste much better, Prophet."

"It is spectacular, Relki," I said. "And I'm not a prophet."

She nodded, and returned to the fire to carve another chunk of meat from the large piece on the spit that they had placed over the fire. She ladled a curved piece of bark full of the stew from the pot on the forked wood and brought it to me.

"Thank you, Relki."

She served each of the others in turn. Salker sat down next to me.

"Relki is a fine cook, Prophet," he said. "She has cooked for many of us in the village. Some of us could survive on our cooking skills, but it would not be pleasant."

I chuckled, "I know what you mean, Salker."

"You spoke of Soulguard, earlier, Prophet," he said. "It is a term that I do not recognize."

"It's the name of a group of people on my world that are like me. We've been keeping the Kresh from controlling our world as they do here. When they would come, we would kill them."

"It is amazing that you can do these things, Prophet," he said. "How is it that there were enough of you to do what you have done?"

"That's a good question, Salker," I answered. "I've been wondering why the Kresh left my world to grow like it did. What I've seen here is a very low technology base."

"You talk of technology," he said. "We are more advanced than many of the other villages here on Kresh. We have a good metal worker, unlike many of the others."

"I'm talking great steps ahead in technology," I returned. "We have weapons that can even hurt the Kresh, not even considering the Soulguard. I wonder if any of the other worlds are any further advanced than the Kresh allow here."

"We have people in our village from twelve different worlds, Prophet," he said. "None have talked of anything more advanced than our own tools."

"I guess you don't have any from Earth," I said. "But you were asking about the Soulguard. Every person has the potential to become a Soulguard. There is some knowledge that a lot of people lack that is needed to do it though."

"Yes?" Salker asked with a gleam in his eyes.

The others had been listening as we talked and ate. They moved closer to hear me better.

"The first thing you need to know is that there is a massive well of power under the surface of the world that feeds all life. Animals, plants, and people. This is fact, tried and true. It's one of the first things you have to accept. There can be no doubt, or it is much harder to succeed in doing what is needed to become a Soulguard."

"Assuming you accept that, the next thing is the connection that feeds each living thing, called a Soulstream."

I placed my hand against my solar plexus, "This is the spot where your stream connects to your Soul. It is in the same place on every person. You can't see it, but it is there. What we do is to alter that stream to feed the body in different spots, to let the body process that life force much more quickly than before. This has effects on the body. Without the body having to distribute the power, there is so much more of it instantly available. You'll be stronger, faster, and heal very quickly from wounds."

"This is hard to just accept, Prophet," The short, dark haired man named Pol said.

"You've seen what I've done," I said. "This is how I did it. The fact that it is so hard to accept is probably why the same thing hasn't already sprang up over here. It takes two things to succeed. Belief and focus. If you don't have both, it's not going to work. Believe me, I was skeptical, even after seeing the Soulguard in action. The first stage is the hardest."

"I see."

"When we get to Redoubt and you get settled in, we can begin some of the focusing exercises I started with."

Pol nodded, but I could see the doubt on his face.

"And what of us, if we can't do what you ask?" Huynini asked. I had learned that the small dark skinned woman cwas Huynini, and Firennia was the tall red-haired woman. "Will we be sent back out?"

"Absolutely not," I said. "There is more to Redoubt than just training to be Soulguard. There'll probably be quite a few without the belief or the focus to do it. Redoubt is a word in my language that means refuge. You'll find that a refuge is exactly what it is."

She nodded. I could see the skepticism in all of them about that statement. They would find out soon enough.

"So you called this animal an olnyaq?" I asked as I took the last bite from my skewer and chewed it. It didn't taste like pork, but not quite beef either.

"Yes, Prophet," Relki answered. "It has a wild taste to it, but when it is raised on grains it removes most of that."

"I've heard similar things about animals back home," I said. "One of the guys I served with used to always buy his meat on the hoof."

There was about another hour of talk before the others found semi-comfortable spots and went to sleep. I stayed awake and kept watch.

Sometime in the night, Salker awoke to take a turn at watch, but I waved him back to his spot. I could see he was still tired, and I didn't need any sleep for days if I didn't want to. I probably wouldn't sleep until we reached Redoubt.

Chapter 12

As the night began to turn to dawn, the others began stirring. I had kept the fire burning through the night to keep them warm. I didn't feel the chill like I did before tying my knot, and even less after the changes that came later. I was used to working with the Soulguards, and had been reminded of that the day before.

The small group began doing a morning ritual of sorts removing most of the traces that we were in the clearing.

"I'm guessing travel is a dangerous prospect?" I asked Salker as he approached.

"Yes, Prophet," he answered. "No one travels unless it is absolutely necessary. The Masters have been known to take travelers, and add them to their slaves."

"I really don't like that term," I said. "Slavery is becoming less and less common on my world."

"It is a normal occurrence here, Prophet."

"With no travel, it must be hard to keep from, how would be a nice way of saying it, too much inbreeding of the population?"

"The Masters have a system for that," he said. "They bring a group of people from other worlds, and leave them in Sargonas every year. We teach them what they need to know to become a part of our village. Each brings new skills to our community, and the Masters sometime take groups from Sargonas, as they did with us. The new villagers are used to fill the empty spaces from which the others were taken."

"Basically everyone lives in fear of being taken at any moment, and sent to slave for the Masters?"

"Or worse, to be taken and eaten in front of other Humans as some sort of message."

"That makes me want to kill them even more," I muttered.

Relki began packing chunks of meat from the olnyaq in the hide of the beast to carry with us, but I saw something I didn't expect near the edge of the clearing. Most animals fled when a Soulguard was near. This one hadn't, which was very surprising.

"We only need enough for a day, Relki," I said. "Leave the rest for whatever that critter over there is. She has some little ones with her."

She looked toward the animal that was just inside the tree line.

"Only a stranger worries that a Kilnyeri is hungry," she said, shaking her head.

The Kilnyeri was about the size of a mid-sized dog but she was covered in a thick coat. Her face looked more like a cat than a dog, perhaps somewhere in between. She just sat there, and watched as our group moved out of the clearing.

As we moved away, she entered the clearing with six small puffs of fur following.

"Damn, that's the cutest critter I've seen in years," I said. "I bet Lyrica would like one as a pet. Make up for that ugly assed dog she has."

"It would take a brave person to want a Kilnyeri for a pet, Prophet," Pol said.

"She looks harmless enough," I said.

"Her looks are deceiving, Prophet," Gers returned. He had been quiet since the party had joined me to return to Redoubt. Gers looked like what I would picture a Viking. Tall, Blonde haired, and blue eyed. His accent was a little different than the others.

"They would have to be, Gers, if she's as dangerous as you guys say."

"My little one asked what a Kilnyeri eats when we first came to Sargonas. The answer we received was that a Kilnyeri eats whatever a Kilnyeri wants to eat," Huynini said. "Later I saw one kill a dogerift. Afterwards, I always say that."

"You have a child?" I asked.

"She is with my Heart Sister, Prophet," she said. "When the Masters come, and take the ones they pick, we have already chosen our Heart Sibling to care for those we can no longer care for."

I stopped, feeling the depth of what these people lived with every day. It sparked my anger, and I wanted to do something about it.

"Worry not, Prophet," Huynini placed her hand on my shoulder. "My Heart Sister is my family. She will care for little Sadyuni as if she were her own. There is no one better to watch over her."

"Mark my words, Huynini," I said. "Your child will be returned to you soon. This I promise."

"Any other person who said that, I would call a liar," she said. "But I saw you slay the Masters with your bare hands. You killed, and brought back an olnyaq across your shoulder with no weapons. I will hold this hope in my heart that you can truly give me back my little one. When we reach this refuge you speak of, I will train, and I will succeed. You will see, Prophet."

She walked past me in the direction we had been going.

"An honorable quest," Salker said as he joined me. "My world loves their quests, Prophet. You would make a good Parlaisian. Do not forget this promise, Prophet."

"I won't, Salker," I said. "I refuse to see anyone lose their child, especially if I can do something to prevent it."

"You lost someone," he said. "I can see it writ on your face."

"Yes, and she is not losing her child."

He nodded, "It is sometimes custom on my world to take a guide when questing in unknown territory. When the time comes, I would like to be your guide, Prophet."

I nodded as we continued toward the sea where Redoubt awaited.

Chapter 13

I stood on the shore looking out into the sea. There was a storm brewing out over the water.

"Jonny," I said, "did you get one of the bots set up to travel in water?"

"Yes, Friend Rictor," he answered.

Jonny had been excited to hear from me, when I had gotten back in range. I think he didn't expect me to come back. It took a lot of guts to help me leave, when he had been alone so long.

"I'm going to bring three of our new friends out in the water inside of a shield bubble. I need you to motor them down to the airlock, while I swim down."

"Yes, Friend Rictor."

I turned back to the group who stood on the beach, "Redoubt is under the water there. I'll take three of you down at a time. I will keep the water from closing in, and you can breathe inside of the bubble. Who goes first?"

Huynini stepped forward. The girl was brave. I could see the fear on her face. Salker and Pol followed.

"I can see you guys are having issues with this, so this is what I'll do. I'll take these three down, and bring Salker back up. He seems to be trusted by all of you."

I could see relief in several of the others.

The three joined me as I retrieved my mask from the duffel. We strode out into the water, and I created a cylindrical shield around them. I held the shield steady as they began to float, and pushed it out into the deeper water. Three metallic arms came from beneath the waves to grip the shield, and pulled it under the water to gasps from those within it. Then I placed the mask over my face, and dove behind them, forming a handle on the top of the shield. I grasped it, and Jonny pulled us down. Lights on the robot lit up the sea under us, and I could see the amazed looks all three cast about themselves. From the depths to the robot, this was all new for these people. Soon after, we entered the airlock, and the robot turned away, withdrawing from the lock.

It cycled closed, and the water began to subside. When the water was gone, I closed the portal that fed the cylinder.

"This looks like some of the buildings in Hub," Salker said.

"It was made by the same people."

The inner door opened.

"Welcome to Redoubt," Jonny Minion said from the com system.

"Let me introduce you to the one who runs this place," I said. "His name is Jonny Minion, and he is Redoubt."

The three of them were staring around at the metallic structures.

"Now, I think we should head back up for the others, before they decide I drowned you all."

Salker returned to the air lock with me, and I reformed the shield around us both. Jonny's robot clamped onto the end as he had done before, and we were pulled from the lock, and pushed toward the surface.

As the light danced through the water, we saw a huge form flash by. It had turned, and fled as soon as it got within range of the sensors that Jonny had been adding since I had left. He was using sonics to drive away the sea life.

"I like this much better, Jonny," I said.

"I would hope so," he returned.

I turned my head toward Salker, "First time I got out in the water, one of those swallowed me."

"How could you survive such a thing?"

"Sometimes you just eat something that doesn't agree with you."

Salker belly laughed, and came dangerously close to a snort.

I liked the way they learned the languages in the old days, but the ancient language was irritating sometimes. They didn't use contractions, and when I would, my speech dropped back into English. Sometimes I caught it, and sometimes I didn't. The others seemed to take it in stride, and work out what I was saying from the rest of the sentence.

I could see the light from above beginning to penetrate the waters shortly before the cylinder broke the surface. Closing the portal, I motioned to the figures on the beach.

Relki and Gers were heading out into the water. I guess they had worked out who was next before we got back.

"You ready?" I asked.

With nods all around, I glanced back out into the water at the storm that was closing in. The next trip would be in rougher waters.

"Be back as quick as I can," I said to Staslin and Firennia. "If you have to retreat to the tree line, do it. I'll come there when I resurface."

Once again the robot snagged the shield, and we descended into the dark water.

When I returned, the wind was whipping the waves into a frenzy, but Firennia and Staslin both huddled on the beach. They came forward quickly, and I opened the shield cylinder around them. The amazement I could see in them, as we sank down, was contagious. I felt the same when I really thought of what we were doing. Descending a thousand feet under water to enter a refuge built ten thousand years ago, possibly to begin building an army to reclaim that ten thousand year old birthright.

Colin was always one to think big, and I figured there were many worse people to choose to follow than Rash'Tor'Ri. As far as building an army in Redoubt, that would depend on a certain Artificial Intelligence.

"Jonny, what say we get our new guests a hot meal, and some new clothes?"

"I will certainly do so, friend Rictor," he said. "I hope our friends like fish. I have harvested a rather large supply since the outer door has been open. They are attracted to the light."

"I am guessing that would be fine, buddy."

Chapter 14

"From what I can gather," I said, "All you have to do is put the headpiece on, and will the machine to start. As you do that, I'll enter the code on this console, and the generators should start up."

"I will do as directed, Prophet."

"Thank you, Relki," I answered. "And I'm not a prophet."

"As you say."

Relki looked much different. The clothing that Jonny provided was tailored to fit each of our new guests, as was the clothing he had given to me. With no need to disguise myself, the clothing was much more modern, or ancient, whichever way you chose to look at it. She wore soft cotton-like pants with a loose, comfortable shirt. Over the shirt was an interesting robe-like garment that was open on the front. She had chosen a turquoise color and it was very nice.

I looked like a dark Jedi from one of Colin's favorite games he had played for years. I gave the boy a lot of crap over his damn Star Wars addiction, but I kind of liked the concept, myself. Although I would never admit it to him, because his head was big enough already.

Relki sat in the chair that reclined in order to bring her head under the silver helmet hanging from the hook inside the machine that looked like a huge MRI tube. It was big enough for the whole chair to slide into.

She reached up, took the helm, and eased it onto her head.

"I am ready, Prophet."

I turned to the console, "Do it."

I began typing the code into the console. As I entered the last digit, the hair stood up on the back of my neck. I heard Relki gasp as she felt what a Mage would feel as they Pulled from the Source. I knew this was what she was feeling, because my teeth began to ache from being so near a Pull of that size. I had felt that same thing so many times.

The Pull began to lose its force as the machines began to work.

"All generators are online, friend Rictor!" Jonny exclaimed in wonder. I was always a little surprised at Jonny's reactions. He acted so human. It was hard to see him as anything other than another Human, when he did things like that.

"Friend Relki," he said. "You can remove the helmet, and leave the machine now that the generators are on. I thank you so much. There are some more things for you to do after I give you some learning imprints. But for now you can join the others if you wish."

Relki looked a little bit dazed as she removed the helm, and slid out of the chair. I was instantly across the room to catch her arm, as her knees gave way when she stood up.

"Thank you, Prophet," she said. "That was just a bit... overwhelming."

"I bet it was," I said with a grin. "I remember when the Boss raised me to a Mage. Hell of a feeling."

"I am alright, now, Prophet," she said. "I will go join the others with the crops."

I nodded as she took a deep breath, stood straighter, and strode out of the room.

"The gardens have been good for our guests, friend Rictor," Jonny said. "They were feeling like they were not doing anything in return for the things we offered."

"I know, my friend," I answered. "I also know you are perfectly capable of taking care of the crops without their help. You did a good thing there to ask them to help. Perhaps we can involve more people in some of that sort of thing as we get more folks down here."

"I think you are right friend Rictor."

"Are you working with them on the focusing techniques?" I asked.

"Yes, they are all doing quite well with focusing, even amidst distraction."

"Very good," I said. "Thank you for helping with that. I need to make another foray topside, and see about returning a child to her mother. Salker and I will be out for several days this time. Have you got some more sensors for me to place in the forest to extend your range?"

"With the boost from the generators, I have a much stronger signal to use, so the sensors will not have to be so close together. I have twenty sensors prepared, if you want to plant them along the way to Sargonas."

"That sounds good to me, buddy," I said. "How far apart will I have to set 'em up?"

"We will have to do some testing as you go, friend Rictor."

"Sounds like a plan."

I started to leave the room but Jonny stopped me.

"Before you go, friend Rictor, there is something I must tell you. I have spoken with all of the refugees from Sargonas. Before, I was afraid to join you in this endeavor you are beginning. I know you promised to bring people back here to stay if I did not wish to join you. After speaking to them, I have discovered a feeling that bothers me greatly. I find that I am angry at the Kresh for making them live as they do. I find myself truly wishing I could do as you do, and hurt them for what they have done to those that created me. I also know I cannot do what you do and hurt them, physically. Therefore I will hurt them in any way that I can."

"I know what you are feeling, Jonny," I said. "I want to be back where I can follow the Boss out into a horde of Kresh, and cut loose with everything I have. I've spent years trying to hurt them for what they do to people on my own world. Then I was brought here by some outrageous twist of fortune, and I see what they did to the whole Human race. I'm outraged, and it burns inside me like a fire that is looking for any way to change it."

"We will build your army, friend Rictor," Jonny said. "We will build it right here in Redoubt. Bring those you wish to train here, and we will train them. Bring those you wish to protect, and we shall protect them."

"Well said, my friend."

"We will need to begin an education program for those you bring to Redoubt," Jonny said. "Much of the knowledge from the Creators was lost, but there is still a small core of knowledge left. To get it, we must add the knowledge of another Gestalt."

"Do whatever you need to, Jonny. Tell me where this one is located, and I'll fetch the memory core for you."

"I can use one of the refugees for this, friend Rictor," he said. "You and friend Salker must begin your quest for friend Huynini."

Chapter 15

Salker and I looked down from a ridge into Sargonas. It seemed that the disappearance of twenty Kresh had earned the notice of others. Unless this was a coincidence.

"The Masters never come this soon after a group has been here," Salker said. "I fear they have come to see what happened to their last group."

"So much for coincidence."

"They will gather a new group to take and we must not interfere, Prophet," He said. "If two groups disappear from the same village there will be repercussions."

"I know, Salker," I said. "It truly galls me to let 'em make off with a bunch more folks though."

The Kresh dragged a woman from the crowd of people in the central plaza of the small village. She held a child in her arms.

"That is not happening," I said.

"What do you wish to do, Prophet?"

"I'm sorry, Salker," I said as I stood up, "But I'm about to interfere."

"Then we interfere," he stated and stood beside me.

The Kresh'Far, or soldier, snatched the child from the woman, and pitched it back toward the crowd. Her screams of terror, as she flew through the air, stopped as I caught her. I had cleared close to five hundred feet in an instant. I slid the child behind me to the ground, and strode forward toward the Kresh.

"I could explain to you what is about to happen, Kresh," I said to the one who had tossed the girl fifty feet from where he had stood. "But I think I'll just show you."

I Pulled, and opened five disc launchers. All five spewed flaming discs of Soulfire into the chest of that single soldier. When I stopped there wasn't much left of the Kresh'Far.

Turning to the rest of the Kresh that stood in utter surprise I said, "Maybe I'll tell you... Ah hell, not worth the effort."

There are times for strategy, and there are times when you just need to do a Rourke. I did a Rourke. I charged in amongst the thirty or so Kresh, and ripped them apart with my bare hands. They were soldiers, and they never even stood a chance.

When I was finished, I turned to find myself facing eighty-three adults and twelve children, who peeked from behind the adults. They were unmoving, as they actually processed what had just happened.

"Salker?" one of the women asked as they saw him stride into the square.

They all seemed to move as one to surround Ruud. Coincidentally, it also took them further away from the remains of thirty-eight Kresh and a bloody Soulmage.

"I gotta start using that shield," I muttered as I tried to wipe some of the Kresh blood from my hands.

***

"They will come to kill us all now!" the Overman exclaimed. "You've killed us all... whatever you are!"

"He is the Prophet of Rash'Tor'Ri," Salker answered. "You will treat him with respect."

"You have no right to speak here, Salker Ruud!" the Overman continued. "You were taken. Your voice carries no weight here."

Salker stood and strode down the aisle to the front of the room, where the red-faced Overman stood.

"On my world, Reegas, I would drag you out the door, and challenge you to a duel," he said. "Here, I will leave it to the people of Sargonas to decide if they would listen to one who has led them for the last twelve seasons, or a blustering windbag who has been Overman for a lunar cycle."

He turned to the people gathered in the large meeting hall, "What say you, people of Sargonas? Will you listen to what I have to say? Or do you wish us to leave you to your fate? It is not a fate you have chosen, but we of Sargonas have always lived or died at the whim of others. The Prophet has shown me a place where we can all go and be safe from the Masters."

"There is no place free of the Masters," a large woman in the front row said. She was probably six and a half feet tall if I was guessing right.

"You are right," I said as I strode to the front of the room. "This world is under the heel of the Kresh. What I can offer you is a place the Kresh have no knowledge of currently. I can offer you the opportunity to learn how to meet them in battle, as I just did, and survive. I can take you to a place where your children will be able to grow up without the risk of dying because a Kresh is irritated."

"You are the reason…!"

The Overman staggered backwards as I turned to him with fire blazing in my eyes. I had seen this many times from the Boss, and I knew how effective it could be.

I turned back to the crowded room, "I have caused this, and I offer you all a place in Redoubt. This is what I can do to make up for what I have caused."

"There is not much choice," the large woman said. "We stay here, and the Masters will kill us all."

She was speaking to the people in the room as she stood up.

"We should go to this Redoubt. Salker Ruud has sworn it is real, and we all know Ruud. He says that the others who were taken are there, including my Staslin. I for one will go."

I could see many nods in the crowd, but there were many who were just angry.

Another woman, the one who had been carrying the child that was snatched away and thrown, stood.

"Is it true that little Huynini is there in this place?"

"She is there," I said. "She is the reason we are here. I swore oath to reunite her with her child, Sadyuni."

"Then it is a good thing you arrived, Prophet of Rash'Tor'Ri," she said. "The child you saved today was Sadyuni."

"Then I will leave you to decide what you want to do," I said. "Salker will tell you what you need to know. He is someone trusted by the majority of you. I will be outside the village disposing of the Kresh. If you choose to stay, there will be no evidence of what transpired here today."

I strode down the aisle to the shabby wooden door, and left the building. I hoped they would come with me, but if they chose not to, the least I could do is clean up the mess. I grabbed the first Kresh body I came to, and dragged it toward the others. Reaching down, I grasped the leg of another, and dragged them both toward the outskirts of the small village

to pass some time, while the made their decisions.

I knew I was asking a lot of these folks. To
leave the only thing they had known, and trust
in a complete stranger. But I had seen something in these people. Even after all of what the
Kresh had done, they were not broken. There
was a spirit in them that had been waiting
thousands of years to be given the chance to
blossom. I had seen it in Salker the first time I
said I could train them. I saw it again in the
woman from the front row.

These people had been through trial after
trial, and I could still see that spirit. That's
what it means to be Human.

As I returned to the pile of bodies, I found
the large woman dragging parts of the bodies
out of the mess, and throwing them in a cart.
Alongside her was the woman who I had seen
with the child.

She nodded, "We will help you, Prophet.
You saved a number of us from slavery to the
Masters. And I will get to hold my Staslin
again. For that, I could never thank you
enough for. My name is Weriona."

She struck her fist to her chest as Salker had
done when I first met him.

I returned the salute, "I am Rictor."

"And I am Odasa, heart-sister to Huynini," She gave me the salute as well.

I nodded and returned it. Then I reached down, and grasped the ridges along the backs of two more bodies, and dragged them easily out of town.

***

Sixty-eight people joined us when we left Sargonas three days later. There were a small number that refused to go.

"When the Kresh come, tell them most of the village died of a sickness from one of the other worlds. Tell them the bodies were burned."

Salker was talking to the villagers that refused to leave.

"What if we just tell them the truth?" asked the Overman, who refused to join us.

"They'll probably kill you for not stopping the rest of us," Salker said.

"Perhaps they will reward us for our loyalty."

Salker shook his head, "You truly are a pathetic thing, Reegas. Tell them whatever you wish. Maybe they will repopulate the village and let you rule them. Good luck."

I kept my silence. Those that stayed would more than likely die. Best case scenario, they would be taken as slaves. The Kresh had sent a second group for the slaves after the first hadn't returned. They would come for more.

Chapter 16

"The two most important things you must have is faith and focus," I said to the group standing before me. "Jonny has been working with you on the focus exercises I showed him. He says you five are very good."

Huynini was at the front of the group. Jonny had reported that she could focus better than any of the others and Salker told me, after returning with Sadyuni, she would believe anything I said. She would need that faith to succeed. After one of them, any one of them, managed to tie that first loop, it would be easier for the rest.

"I tied my Soulguard knot almost fifty years ago. I was a Marine and used to following orders. They told me it was possible. They showed me the results of doing it. Then they showed me how to do it. This is all I can do for you. You've seen the strength I wield, the speed at my disposal. A Soulguard can attain most of what you have seen."

"Not all?" Salker asked. He had seen the disk launchers in use at Sargonas.

"The launchers are from the changes that Rash'Tor'Ri caused when he ascended me to a Mage. There are other things that I gained from something Jonny did when I showed up here. I don't even know the full repercussions from that. What you will gain is great strength, speed, and a much faster ability to heal. You will not suffer from sickness anymore. Then you will learn to fight."

He nodded.

I reached out about sixteen inches from my body and placed my hand, as if I was grasping a three inch cable right in front on my solar plexus.

"There are four steps to the first loop of the knot," I pointed with my other hand. "First is to grasp the stream with your mind, right here."

"Then grasp the stream right here," I said, placing the other fist as if I were grasping a cable about a foot from my body. "It helps to use the hands as if you are grasping it to keep your mind focused on those points."

"With the closer hand you will pull the stream to your opposite shoulder," I demonstrated with my closer hand. "Then you will pull the stream where your outer hand is holding back in to your solar plexus. This will always keep your stream in the same place when you reach for the next loop."

Huynini had her hands in the proper spots, but nothing was happening when she moved the hands.

"This step takes longer than any of the others. Once you have done this loop you will feel the difference. Faith is no longer an issue, then. Just focus."

I could see the frustration all of them were feeling.

"Very few Soulguards found that spot where faith and focus reach the perfect level the first time they tried. Many have taken months. You must focus past the excitement, past the frustration and..."

"Blessed child of the gods!" Huynini almost fell over as her stream touched her shoulder.

I was there, immediately, "Don't lose the grasp on the other part. Pull it in to you."

She pulled her hand back to her abdomen. I could see the whites of her eyes as she looked back up from her abdomen to stare at me.

"Truly a Prophet," was all she said, and turned to the others who had all lost their focus and crowded around her.

I stepped back from the group to let them see for themselves. This would do them more good than any instruction I could give them.

She staggered, and tripped as she tried to step forward. She was far from a Soulguard, yet. But her strength would have probably doubled as her body was fed from two spots instead of one. Her right arm would be immensely stronger while the rest would still gain from the second connection to the Soulstream.

The Boss had described what he saw when we had been at one of the classes a few years back. The right side of the body, or left, if that is where the second stream connected would shine much brighter and there would be two looping Streams from the solar plexus and the shoulder.

I had never seen anyone tie their stream that quickly. Salker was right, faith was not an issue with Huynini.

Huynini picked Salker Ruud up by the belt and shirt to rounds of laughter from the others.

I decided to let them play. The more they saw of the results, the less that faith would be an issue with the rest of them.

"I told you I would succeed, Prophet," Huynini said as she stumbled from the crowd.

"That you did, Huynini."

"What is the next step, my Prophet?"

"Now you get used to your added strength," I said. "You can hurt someone without meaning to. Once you are adapted to it, we will do some more."

"Yes, My Prophet."

"I ain't a Prophet."

"As you wish."

I just shook my head, "Head to the Fitness Center, and get used to your new abilities. You want to get a good handle on it before interacting with the kid."

"Yes, my Prophet."

I watched the girl stumble toward door at the back of the room with a sigh. I feared I would be stuck with the "Prophet" thing.

"As for the rest of you," I said, turning around, "That is the first time I ever saw someone get the first loop of the knot in that short of a time. Let's see if we can get a couple more."

Chapter 17

I looked over the top of the ridge at the enormous city across the plain from me.

"Damn, Jonny," I said. "That place is huge."

"According to the data from the memory core of TRE2345466JF, Hub was the home of forty-two million humans before the uprising."

"And this one is the one that goes to Doran?"

"Yes friend Rictor."

It would be a small feat to run across that distance, and plunge through that shimmering Gate I could see through the open back panel of the Facility. But I had people depending on me, and I couldn't leave them behind after I had made the promises that I did.

I heard a commotion from off to the left of me. Turning, I saw a group of people running frantically down the valley behind me. Then I saw the Kresh. They were toying with the people. I remembered how they had toyed with my platoon in Viet Nam. All but a few of us died in that nightmare.

Weighing the fact that this was a recon mission against the fact that those people were dying really didn't take long. I had to act, and it had to be fast. There were ten Kresh soldiers. Most of them were bunched together, laughing at the actions of the other three that would circle the Humans and run through to knock one sprawling. Or worse.

I dropped into a focused awareness, and the world slowed to a crawl. I hadn't been as precise with my launchers as some of the Mages that Colin had ascended, but I was pretty sure I could get those three.

I launched myself through the air with a crunch of collapsing dirt behind me. Then I opened up with the launchers. I used five launchers and only missed with two. Plenty to pick off the three outliers.

Then I landed in the middle of the seven others. It was short work, but I had no idea how long it would take for one of them to send a message with their telepathy. And no idea of the range. The Humans ran onward, around the bend in the trail.

They were no longer in the crosshairs, so to speak, but they were nowhere near safe either. Without my people trained, I couldn't afford to get caught this close to Hub. I had needed to see it for myself.

It had been fourteen days travel to reach Hub from Redoubt. Fourteen days for a Mage. Could I keep a party of Humans that large alive for the month or more it would take to travel back?

"I have to let it go," I mumbled.

"Let what go, friend Rictor?"

"I can't bring that many people across that distance, yet."

"How many?"

"Looked like fifty or so."

"Estimated two and a half lunar cycles for a party of Humans to travel the distance from your position, friend Rictor."

"Have to let it go," I said. "It galls me to do it, though. This whole damn world is screwed up. Everywhere, people are dying and I can't do anything."

"You have already done much, friend Rictor. You have brought over a hundred people to Redoubt. They are safe from the Kresh. You have twenty-eight who have tied their streams at some level or another. Ten of those have completed your 'Soulguard' knot, despite their refusal to swear the Oath you put before them."

"Yes," I said. "I worry a little about that. I've seen what Human nature truly is on my world. The Kresh are doing no more than my own people have done to one another on Earth. That is why the Oath was created."

"But they have a valid argument as well," another voice added.

"I know they do, Reaman," I returned. "Doesn't make me worry less. I understand it, but I still worry."

Reaman was one of the alternate personalities that Jonny had created in his lonely exile. He had finally accepted that they were there, even if he had created them.

"It was proven when the Kresh returned to Sargonas," Jonny said. "Reegas wasted no time before telling his masters about us."

"I guess it is a good thing he didn't know where we were."

"Very true," Reaman replied.

"How are the newest recruits coming along?" I asked.

"The one called Belinia is doing quite well," Jonny answered. "Most of them are improving faster than you had projected."

"It doesn't surprise me after I saw four of the first group tie their first loop on the first day. That is unheard of."

"Perhaps the 'faith' you speak of is harder to attain on your world."

"That could be," I said. "Knowledge is a wonderful thing, but it does become counter-productive to accepting something on faith."

"Perhaps they believe in their Prophet."

"Damnit, Jonny, don't you go drinking the Kool-Aid too."

"I do not know what Kool-Aid is, friend Rictor," he answered. "And I am highly unlikely to drink anything."

"Smart ass," I said with a chuckle. "What do you think the odds are that I can get into that city undetected? Maybe get on the rooftops or something?"

"Less than one percent chance of going undetected, friend Rictor."

"Guess this is as close as I get for now."

"That would be advisable."

"Well, I guess I'll head back to Redoubt," I said. "It's time to start some serious weapon training with some recruits."

"Will you be speaking in any of the villages along the way?"

"I doubt it," I said. "I need to get some of these trained up enough to join me on recon missions. Have to get them some experience out in the field. Then I'll hit the recruitment trail again."

"If you change your mind, my drones have marked ten more villages at various points between you and Redoubt."

"Alright. Keep me posted if any of those look like they need a visit."

"Will do, friend Rictor."

"Thanks Jonny."

"You are welcome friend Rictor."

We had been speaking in English for the most part during our conversation. I no longer needed to use the imprint to speak the language of this world, but I had to consciously choose to do so when I wanted to. It was all there, available if I needed it. That would have been useful when I was learning several languages during my career as a Marine.

Jonny had asked me to teach him my language not long after I arrived, and as soon as the imprint would allow me to use both languages, I had done so.

"How are the swords coming along?" I asked.

"I have fabricated a thousand of them at this time, friend Rictor. I have also completed four hundred sets of the armor you requested. They are strong but they will not stop a Kresh from clawing through."

"They'll be a lot tougher when a Guard is wearing 'em."

"I have seen this when you demonstrated the armor for the others. Friends Salker and Huynini were quite impressed with the difference."

"They'll like it even better when I show them how to make a personal shield. I have no doubts those two will have the focus to build it whether any of the others do or not."

"I agree," Jonny replied. "Reaman had an idea that could make those shields much easier. He suggested a holographic representation of the shield that the person could use to help focus in the right place."

"That could speed up things quite a bit," I said. "Good thinkin', Reaman."

"Thank you," the other voice returned.

Chapter 18

"That man is a beast," I said.

Salker Ruud was sparring with Pol, and it was obvious that Ruud was trained in the use of a sword. He was obviously holding back so the younger man could learn from the sparring.

I'd watched a lot of guards as they learned to use their enhanced speed over the years. Many would have just taken Pol down. Salker paced himself with his opposite, and Pol learned from the experience.

I waited until the two were finished before approaching, "I want you training the others, Salker. It's obvious you're well trained and they can use some of that."

"This, I will do, Prophet."

"And if you need a challenge, I'll be glad to spar with you."

"It would be an honor," he answered. "I have been using the sword from my sixteenth year. Ours are a bit longer, but these are quite useful when using both hands."

"The man is the weapon," I said. "The sword is just an extension."

"Well said," he returned with a grin. "Shall we have a round or two?"

"Certainly," I answered. "May I use those, Pol?"

He handed me the twin practice swords that Jonny had created from a polymer that weighed the same as the steel swords he'd made for us.

As we faced off in the practice ring, others began making their way over to watch.

"Say when, Jonny," I said.

"Three... Two... One," Jonny said. "Begin."

As he had counted, I dropped into the focused state where the world seemed to slow down. When Jonny said to begin, I could see Salker moving much slower than I could move. I met his attack with a strong defense. I would let him work at those defenses for a while.

"You have much training, Prophet," he said as he moved through several attacks.

"Been usin' these things for close to fifty years," I answered. "And I have an advantage in speed."

Salker went low, and almost made it through my guard.

"I have a few secrets, it seems," he said.

"I haven't seen that one before."

"You are not trying, Prophet."

"We'll test your defenses in a few moments, Salker," I said. "The more you train your focus, the faster you will be able to move. You aren't using full speed yet. You'll see as the focus exercises become easier."

We continued for close to half an hour, using both defense and offense. Salker gave me a better workout than I'd seen since arriving in Redoubt. I learned several moves that I had never seen. Perhaps it was because he trained to fight Humans, and I had trained to fight Kresh.

He learned some things just as important. They'd never even contemplated fighting the Masters, so some of the things I took for granted had never even crossed their minds as they trained on Parlais.

As we left the practice ring, I saw Huynini in the track area running. She was fast. The ability to dodge obstacles at high speeds was pretty important, and the track was littered with various pieces. Jonny had placed some of his unused robots all through the area with newly built padding around them. He could move them as he saw fit, and would constantly place them in different spots.

"The girl is fast," Salker said. "She is getting better with the swords as well."

"I know," I said. "I swear she reminds me of a friend of Rash'Tor'Ri's. Quick and deadly."

"With enough weapon training, she will be."

"That's where you come in, my friend," I said with a grin. "Saying that makes me a happy man, Salker. You have no idea how happy I am to give that to you."

"You do not like training," he said. "I have watched you. Although, you are good at it."

"It's the 'Prophet' thing," I said. "I saw this same sort of thing when the boy started makin' waves back home. I'm guilty of it myself. I knew that boy was destined for somethin' big. I followed right along because he needed me to start with. But then I found I needed him just as much. I'd begun to lose my way, Salker."

"That boy showed me somethin'. He'd stand up to anyone, if he was in the right. He stood up to the strongest Mage in the world without knowing how to do any of the big things he can do now. He has a persistent ob-session with the truth, and believes in true jus-tice."

"Gave this old warrior a new way to go," I continued.

"You miss your friend, do you not?" Salker asked. "Did you not think of sneaking into Hub and crossing back over while you were there?"

"I did think about it, Salker," I said. "But then I asked myself what would he do? He'd follow through on what he promised. I can do no less. There's a whole world of injustice right here, and it's time someone started set-ting it right."

"I am glad you stayed, Prophet," he said. "You've given us something we had all but lost."

"What's that?"

"Hope, my friend."

Chapter 19

"These things are impressive, Jonny."

"Thank you, friend Rictor," he returned through my coms.

I was floating a short distance from the air-lock. Jonny had fabricated several new toys for me. I had a set of tanks that would run on the same principle as the facemask he had made me earlier. I could regulate how much air would be generated so that I could float at any particular level I chose.

I wore enough weight to make up for my natural buoyancy, so the added air would raise me, or I could purge the tanks and sink.

That was only one of the new toys. The other was a set of contact lenses. They were connected to the com system, and Jonny could show me an image that overlaid my regular sight. While within range of the proper sensors, I could see a pattern of energy flows in that image.

"This is what Colin can see all the time," I mused.

"Rash'Tor'Ri can see the flows of the Nexus?" Jonny asked.

"That's one of his many abilities," I said. "The Soulguard has another classification for him. Soullord. There used to be a couple on earth back, when the Soulguard was formed. Then thirty or so years back, the Kresh tried to wipe out the last in the bloodline of one of those. They failed. And in failing, they corrupted an unborn baby with their DNA."

"I have heard the others speak of a clan that did experiments to create people with Kresh DNA. They are terrified of them. They call them the Shak'Tar," Jonny said. "Why are you laughing, friend Rictor?"

"They don't need to fear the Shak'Tar anymore, Jonny," I said. "A little while back there was a change in management."

"What do you mean, friend Rictor?"

"Well, as I was saying, they corrupted the DNA of this child. But his genetics were what you might call the 'Perfect Storm'. He grew to have, not only the skills of one of the long lost Soullords, but the mental strength of one of those Kresh'Farrara'Ti."

"Truly?"

"I saw it for myself, Jonny. They sent the Shak'Tar after us on Earth after he killed so many at the Gate in Kansas. They got to some good people before we finally located their base. He used that mental thing they call the Mark, and took the Shak'Tar's Master. When the rest of us got down to the base, they were all kneeling, except that Kresh'Farrara'Ti. He killed himself before allowing a Human to be his Master."

"I would like to relay this conversation to the others if it is alright, friend Rictor. It will be a great relief to them to know that the Shak'Tar are no longer a threat to them."

"By all means, tell them all. Later, after we finish out here, we'll have a 'Campfire', and I can answer any questions. There's a lot that hasn't been said. These folks agreed to follow me, and I follow him. Perhaps it would be good to talk about him for a bit. And the second Soullord that showed up about twenty years after him. That one is named Lyrica Jayne, and, if I don't miss my guess, she has completely stolen that boy's heart."

"I have witnessed the interactions between Humans, what you call love. Friends Weriona and Staslin are never far apart."

"They got a hell of a shakeup when Staslin was taken. Loss like that changes a person. They got a second chance, and they're stronger for it, I think," I said. "If I'd gotten that second chance..."

My voice just faded as I thought of my long dead wife and son, "A second chance would have had me latched to her side for the rest of my life."

"Would that a Gestalt could feel that love, friend Rictor," he said. "But part of it is chemical reactions that a Gestalt just does not have."

"Before the both of us get all maudlin, and have to go get drunk, let's see if we can make this damn thing."

"Agreed, friend Rictor. I do not like to contemplate the fact that I am the only Gestalt left."

"Perhaps there are others out there, buddy," I said. "If so, we'll find 'em."

"Thank you, friend Rictor."

"Alright, let's get to it."

I started weaving a shield that connected to a new secondary airlock Jonny had built with this very thing in mind. The lock was six feet in diameter, so the shield was the same. I slowly wound my way out of the main doors, and began to elevate the shield tunnel at about thirty degrees. The contacts with the image overlay were the only thing that made this possible. There was no way I could have focused this much without being able to see what I was building.

"This is how he makes all the best stuff," I muttered. "Just wait 'til I get to work on the weapons."

"Weapons?"

"Sorry, Jonny," I chuckled. "Talkin' to myself again."

"Understood, friend Rictor," he answered. "It is why I created Reaman and the others."

I laughed, and kept working on the shield that corkscrewed upwards. It took two and a half hours before I reached the surface where I found a rock outcropping that was the proper height above the water to end the shield.

"Now for the really fun part," I said. "Seen him do it dozens of times."

"What, friend Rictor?"

"This."

I slammed the end of the shield tendril of power into the Source, and watched the power surge through the shield.

3...2.. I was hit by the surge before I expected it. The power of the Source felt ridiculously good, as I felt like I was holding the power of some ancient god in my hands.

I connected the second tendril to the Source, and cut the link. Then I released the massive amount of Soulfire into the sky.

"Friend Rictor!"

"I'm ok Jonny."

"Your Nexus energies were higher than I have ever seen in a Human. That should have killed you."

"Probably so, Jonny," I answered. "Whatever you did to me, did something I haven't even seen the Boss do. Never seen him holding in that much power. Not sayin' he couldn't, just never seen it."

I shook my head in wonder, "Send me a couple of recruits up here, Jonny."

Chapter 20

"Is it safe?" Belinia asked as she looked into the dark tunnel that had emerged as Jonny pumped water out.

I stood beside her and looked into the hole, "Let's find out."

I pushed her in.

I heard a yell that turned into laughter somewhere about half way as she cork-screwed down the water slicked surface.

"I hope you have all the water out, Jonny," I said.

"I do, Friend Rictor."

"Good," I returned. "You have one on the way."

I turned to find Yarnust Krole standing with his hand out, "I will leap into the dark hole of my own volition, Prophet."

I laughed, and waved him on.

Krole was one of the people that had come in with Belinia's group. The various villagers tended to stick together as they became adapted to the training.

Krole, like so many of the folks in the villages looked strikingly different from Belinia and her father. The Kresh pulled people from fourteen worlds. They were scattered amongst the thousands of villages across the continent. I had no idea how many people were scattered around Fhlo'Saa'Gellis. When I thought in those numbers the task looked nigh impossible. My small force, here in Redoubt versus a whole world of Kresh.

Krole leapt into the hole and slid out of sight.

"That looks like it could be fun," I said. "When do you think you'll get the portal up and running?"

"We have a single person with the proper genetics, friend Rictor," Jonny answered. "I do not have the information yet to do it. Plus I think I need more generators online, before I can power the portal. We are adding another Gestalt memory core today. Perhaps it is the one with the information we need to use it. It takes me some time to absorb the complete core of a Gestalt."

"It's fine, Jonny," I said. "I'm curious how useful it will be. Like can it be set to go any-where else? Or is it set for one spot only? That will tell how useful it is to us in the long run."

"Perhaps BNN0987LKJ will contain the information we seek."

"Perhaps," I said. "But this will help until we get it going. I would love to be able to put a squad up here a lot faster than we can right now."

"I have begun the construction of the new elevator shaft," he said. "It could take some time to get it completed. It will be in the water for the majority of the distance, but will enter the ground at some point to be accessible from land."

"As long as we have a failsafe, where we can blow it if it is needed."

"It is designed to be able to blow at a moment's notice, friend Rictor."

"We have to keep it hidden well," I said. "We get caught, and it's a repeat of the original Humans down there. Stuck, hiding in a hole."

"Perhaps, friend Rictor," he returned. "But the builders didn't plan as you have. You have access to the water and can travel under the surface if need be."

"True," I said. "But they have the numbers to bottle us up if they ever really chose to."

"Sadly, you are right, friend Rictor."

"I know."

"Do you wish to try out your new entrance?"

"Go ahead and flood it, Jonny," I shook my head. "Send me up Huynini's squad. We're goin' out to try a new village, and I think it's time for them to get their feet wet."

"I will have them on the surface as soon as they prepare for the journey. Which village do you intend to visit?"

"I'm thinkin' one twenty-three," I said. "It's not too big and doesn't have a good crop system according to the drone images. They'll have a rough time of it this season. Maybe they'll prefer to join us."

"Perhaps they will."

"Kill two birds with one stone. Gain recruits, and help keep a village from starving. I'd like a supply drop from one of the drones, if they choose not to come with us, so have Salker put a package together to help get them through."

"Will do, friend Rictor."

"Nothing that can be considered too high tech, so none of the prepacked stuff. I'm sure Salker can tell from some of the images what should be needed. He ran Sargonas for a good spell."

"I'm sure he will be able to put together something," he said. "I would like to send a sensor platform with you to place atop the mountain range that overlooks one twenty-three. I could use a drone for sensors but you are going there anyway..."

"Sure," I said. "Send it up with First Guard."

"She is quite proud of the name they chose for her."

"That she is," I said with a smile. "She deserves it, though. I never saw a Guard knot their stream that quick."

"None of the others have matched her," he said.

"I know," I returned. "The girl has a drive that most people, whether they are here or back on my world, can't match."

"The First guard's Squadron is entering the airlock, friend Rictor."

"They didn't waste any time."

"They rarely do," he answered.

"True enough," I said. "I'll do inspection when they get here."

The new drone Jonny had built could carry ten people to the surface at a time without using my shields. I didn't want them trapped inside during the times I was gone on recruitment missions.

The squadron was only a group of five at the moment, but they would be twenty-five, when we had the members to fill it out. We had three squads of five who had tied their streams completely.

Salker was the Guard Captain of Squad Two and Weriona was Guard Captain of Squad Three. She had jumped right into the training when she arrived, and had found her place in the scheme of things. She and Staslin were both destined for a Captain position, but he would remain with Salker's Squad until then.

As more Guards entered our Redoubt, more Squadrons would be added. I would love to see a hundred thousand Guards scattered across this world. A million. Hell, I'd love to see the whole population of Humans with Soulguard knots. I'd heard Colin say the same thing many times, but never really felt that way until I came here, and saw the lives my race had to live on Fhlo'Saa'Gellis.

Maybe I'd started feeling that way about Earth after First Kansas. Definitely felt that way after New York. But this world really drove those feelings in deep. I would see it spread as far as I could, until we took this world back, or they brought me down in battle.

Chapter 21

"First Guard," I called out.

"Yes, my Prophet?"

I grimaced. I hated being called a Prophet. But I think I may be stuck with it.

I turned to face the Squad that had followed me the last three days. Huynini stood proudly at the front of that squad.

"You've all done a great job since this squad was formed," I said. "It's time for a test of sorts. I want you to go down there and recruit. I'm not here, and this is your mission. You know what we are about. Show these folks. Let them know it."

Huynini nodded, "We will not fail you, my Prophet."

I shook my head as I watched the five of them walk down to the village where several young men were clearing a section of forest. It was close to the edge of the village, but I could see several, partially finished, dwellings. They were probably cutting timber to build the houses.

Everything these people did was so much harder than it was on Earth with our advanced technology. A sawmill would be a beautiful thing to the people using axes to notch logs for their buildings.

I didn't enhance my hearing. I just watched as First Guard Squadron approached the men. As Huynini introduced herself, I could see the men keep looking to Pol or Dalinis, both of the males of the group.

Huynini continued explaining to the men. Finally she stopped, and cocked her head a little to the side. She held a finger up as if to say "Wait" and picked up the long handled, double bladed axe they had been using. She held it by the end of the handle, and raised it in her right hand with ease.

I could tell she was concentrating on the axe, and grinned as the handle began to glow. She pushed her Soul outward through her hand to imbue the axe with Soulfire. None of the new Guards had managed that yet. It seemed she would earn that title of First Guard once more as the axe began to burn with the power of her Soul.

She held it up in front of the men who were completely focused on her. Then she walked over to a tree, and swung the axe with her single hand to impact the tree. The tree shuddered as splinters exploded from the other side. Then it slowly toppled and fell with a loud crunch.

I chuckled as she turned back to begin talking to the men, who were giving her their utmost attention. I was still chuckling as I turned and strode back into the trees.

"Seems she has that well in hand," I muttered.

First Guard Squad came back after several hours in the small village with no less than twenty-five volunteers. Fifteen of them were women. I figured Huynini had gotten herself a few fans.

"We had to refuse a few of the volunteers, My Prophet," she said as she returned to the tree line. "Not everyone would come, so we could not take all of the able bodies from the village."

"Good call, First Guard," I returned. "We don't want to hurt their chances of surviving the cold season. Did you tell them about the supplies that will be coming?"

"I did," she answered. "They were very appreciative. There were hardly any who spoke against us as Reegas did in Sargonas."

"I would say this is a great success," I said. "Now you need to take your squad off in that direction."

I pointed away from the direction we had come into the area.

"Yes, my Prophet," she returned. "Might I ask what you wish?"

"Girl, you have to catch some critters before they get too far out of range. We have to feed twenty-five extra people on the way back. And you can bet they'll be beating feet in that direction to get away from us."

First Guard Squad didn't let me down, though. It may have taken them an hour to catch up with the fleeing animals but they came back with four olnyaq draped over four shoulders. The other carried a sack of some sort of root he had recognized.

Later that evening, as we stopped for the night to camp, I found out they tasted a lot like a sweet potato.

The villagers had made short work of making the meat travel friendly. A small, swarthy fellow named Bigosa had built a sort of box where he kept a fire burning as he hung a good part of the meat to smoke overnight.

I was halfway through a hunk of olnyaq meat when I heard something that sounded extremely familiar. Looking up from the chunk of meat, I saw one of the new recruits playing something that looked interesting.

"You like the Cantumoor, Prophet?" the young man asked.

"It looks a lot like what my people call a guitar," I said. "Do you mind?"

I motioned to see if I could hold it.

"Of course, Prophet," he said and held it out to me. "You can play?"

"I can do a little with a guitar," I returned. "This looks to have an extra string. I think I can make do."

I sat back in front of the fire, and strummed a little to get the feel of it. Very close to guitar. I strummed a few notes.

"Do you sing, my Prophet?"

"I only know a few in English," I said. "Perhaps when Jonny gets the program up for Implants of English."

"Several of us have learned a bit of English," Jaharis, one of First Guard Squad said.

"Go ahead and play a song for them, Prophet," the young man I had borrowed the instrument from said. "I will sing for the rest of us after."

I nodded and started playing a tune I loved. You couldn't beat Johnny Horton for a ballad.

I could almost put the right voice to the tune, and did a close cover of Sink the Bismark.

As soon as I mentioned ships, Jaharis perked up. I could even see the crestfallen look as the Hood went down fighting the Bismark. He actually cheered as the song finished, and the British fleet sank the German battleship.

When I was done First Guard Squad all applauded as well as some of the newcomers. I smiled and handed the Cantumoor back to the young man who loaned it.

"Thank you..."

"Peligios," he said. "Very well done, Prophet."

"I appreciate the support, Peligios. I managed but I'm no professional."

"You play as well as the one who taught me the chords, Prophet. You are very good."

"Go on and play something from here for us, Peligios," I said. "I'd love to hear some of it. I haven't heard any music since I left my world."

Peligios began to strum the Cantumoor. The melody he started was interesting. He made use of that extra string that I had just skipped over as I played. He began to sing, and I could tell the boy had spent a lot of time with the music he played. He was good.

The rest of the evening went like that, and quite a few evenings after. We would sit and listen to Peligios, as he sang and played.

Chapter 22

"Is it true you have ships on your world made from iron with guns so big, Prophet?" Jaharis asked as we entered the clearing along the coast where the entrance to Redoubt waited.

"Much bigger guns than those, nowadays," I said. "That was eighty years ago when we fought in World War Two. There are much bigger guns on our ships now."

"You have spoken of battles with the Masters," he said. "Did you use those guns?"

"We spent years fightin' with the Kresh in caves and such because they were doin' their thing in secret. When it all blew up, and we went to war with 'em in the open, it was in highly populated areas. I would love to have dropped some bombs on their asses, and see how they liked it, but we would have killed our own along with the Kresh."

"They flooded thousands of Kresh into New York, right in the middle of a city of eight million people."

His eyes widened at the numbers. Sometimes I get surprised by what the folks over here know. The majority have a minimum amount of education. Many haven't been taught much more than what it took to survive. Then there were folks like Jaharis. I could tell he was more adept with numbers, and he could write with ease. He had been quiet about his past, and I only knew he was from Krongis. And he was a devil with a sword.

"My Enclave held twenty thousand," he said. "It is hard to imagine eight million people."

"It was a handful cleaning that place out. The one weakness we discovered in those that attacked us was their overpowering hatred of Rash'Tor'Ri. We were looking at a long, drawn out campaign to get them all until he placed himself out in the middle of 'em and let them know he was there."

"Alone?"

"Nope," I said. "He took Lyrica Jayne with him. You put those two together, and it's like a hurricane and an earthquake combined to make the perfect disaster."

"I have seen the storms you call hurricanes," he said. "Most of Krongis is ocean. We have many of those in the warmer season. But

I have never seen the land shake as you describe."

"I spent most of my time with feet planted firmly on the ground," I said. "When the ground underfoot rolls like the ocean waves, it is terrifying."

"I could see that," he said as he stepped harder on the ground ahead of him. "It would, indeed, be terrifying."

"You have told us of Rash'Tor'Ri, but who is this Lyrica Jayne?"

"I can't believe I haven't talked about her," I said, shaking my head. "Anything that involves him has to involve her. He discovered her in Tennessee back before the whole mess went public. She's like him in most ways. She can manipulate the Source like he does. The difference comes from the Kresh DNA he carries. She doesn't have that. Hell, she doesn't need it to be a force of her own."

"I would love to be able to go there and see all of these wonders you talk of, Prophet."

"One day, Jaharis, perhaps you will."

He was quiet for a few moments before turning toward me.

"I had given up hope of ever returning to Krongis," he said. "I was about to do the honorable thing, and take my life before the Kresh could learn of what we have built on Krongis. Then you walked into our village. I saw a chance that I might live on. Then you told us of the Shak'Tar falling to Rash'Tor'Ri, and I knew I could stay alive to fight. Now I see a glimmer of hope to see this mighty Navy you talk of. It never stops surprising me."

"What's that?"

"The hope you have brought to this miserable world. Look around you at the people you have brought back. You can see the hope of a future almost radiating from them. That is what you have already done here. When we have the numbers to truly reach out to the distant lands, and show that hope to the rest of this world, you will be amazed."

"I'm just doin' the best I can for my people," I said. "It took me two wars, forty years as a Soulguard, and getting blown into a new world to truly find where I belong. Earth was my world, true, but I feel like I found my people here on another world. I can do my best to show my people what it means to be free."

"And that is where the hope comes from," he said.

"Welcome back, Friend Rictor," Jonny said as we approached the water line.

"Glad to be back home, Jonny," I said. "Scouts out! Clear the area before we open the door."

"Yes Sir!" First Guard Squad scattered.

"I have drones in range, friend Rictor," Jonny said. "There are no interlopers."

"It's a good exercise for the squads," I said. "They should always clear the area before coming in. No telling whether there will always be drones in range."

"It is a good plan, friend Rictor," he returned. "Shall I begin draining the tube or shall I wait until they all report back?"

"We'll wait for them," I answered. "Standard practice. Always clear the area first."

"I have successfully assimilated the Memory Bank for HRG7687656LKM, friend Rictor. I was unsure what he was responsible for but now I have something to show you. There was a satellite facility I was completely unaware of. He was responsible for building it."

"What's in it?"

"The Makers stored something they considered too dangerous to leave in the main facility. It is located at the bottom of the trench that you can see as you leave the main hatch. It is one thousand, three hundred, and four feet below this facility."

"That sounds interesting," I said. "That's the next thing on my agenda, then. I want to see what it is."

"I figured you would," he said. "I admit, I'm quite curious to see it as well."

The final scout returned to declare an all clear. Huynini leaped to the top of the rock outcropping.

"Drain the tube, Jonny," I said and joined her at the top.

She was staring down into the hole as the water began to recede at a quick rate.

"You made this with a shield?" she asked.

"Yep, with a little help from Jonny."

"Astonishing," she returned. "How do you stand inside of it at that steep an angle?"

"Go check it out," I said and pushed her in.

There was a short yelp from her before I turned back to the group of people who were watching with various expressions. The newcomers, for the most part, were startled. First

Guard Squad, well, most of them were laughing. Those that weren't were doing a good job of holding in the laughter.

"It seems Huynini, our First Guard, has decided to greet you at the bottom of the slide. There are four ladies here with small children. I would like each of the rest of the squad to accompany them as they slide. It would help with the children I think."

I looked at the group, "So, who would like to go first?"

Chapter 23

The darkness was pierced by the bright lights from Jonny's drone as I let it pull me down into the trench.

"There is probably a security code for entrance, friend Rictor," he said. "There is also a maintenance code that the Gestalt had in his core program. We can use it to enter the facility. According to the records, the facility has an airlock. Why would they design something like this, and not have one for the facility where they trapped themselves?"

"Doesn't make any sense," I said. "What if the storage facility was there first? Maybe they located the redoubt close to it because it was there first. It would make better sense than building the facility after and not having any way to escape the one they were in."

"Perhaps," he answered. "It is frustrating to have tiny pieces of the knowledge held by the Gestalts I absorb. The barest of hints as to what happened. I was there, but all I saw were my duties. If I could see all of their memories, I could piece everything together. Instead, we have more questions."

"The study of history has always been that way, Jonny," I said. "I used to teach History at a local college back before…"

My voice just sort of faded off.

"Before what, friend Rictor?"

"Well… Before I took a different path."

"I find it quite fulfilling to teach," Jonny said. "I was unaware of this feeling until I began teaching groups of our friends languages and focusing drills. I find I truly enjoy it."

"Once upon a time, I did too," I said. "I looked forward to the day I could teach my son."

"You have a son, friend Rictor?"

"I almost did, Jonny. I almost did."

"I have become much more intuitive since I have Humans with me again, friend Rictor," he said. "If you wish to talk, I will listen. I will not push you on the matter."

I nodded. Jonny was swiftly becoming my closest friend. He didn't buy into the "Prophet" nonsense. He knew exactly where I came from and what I wanted to do.

"I'll tell you about them sometime, Jonny," I answered. "Preferably with enough alcohol to actually affect a, whatever I would be classified as."

I saw the light ahead reflect from the surface of something, "I see it, Jonny. How does it stay that clean, I wonder?"

I was looking at a pristine metal surface.

"Have you not noticed how clean my drones stay?" he asked. "The metal used by the Makers is hard to sully. It does not corrode over time, I am happy to say. Imagine a Gestalt, with a corroded core. It would not be a good thing."

"True enough," I grinned.

We stopped a few feet from the shiny surface, "I will have the drone send the maintenance code."

Nothing happened for a few moments. Then the surface moved sideways to open a chamber on the other side. It was a large chamber so the drone entered with me. The door slid shut once more, and I heard the pumps begin to drain the chamber.

The drone extended a probing sensor up out of the water.

"Nothing harmful is detected friend Rictor," Jonny said. "The air is safe to breath."

I pushed the release on the facemask just before the water dropped below it. The air smelled clean. Cleaner than the air in Redoubt.

Of course there weren't hydroponics and a hundred and fifty people in the storage facility. Life has a smell and there was no smell here.

When the room was empty the inner wall slid to the side. Lights brightened slowly to a clear light, much like florescent lighting without the flicker and hum.

The chamber on the other side of the airlock wasn't very big and I could see no doors in the smooth surface of the round wall. In Redoubt, the doors were inset a fraction so they were discernable. In the center of the room was a pedestal of sorts.

"I cannot tell what it is, friend Rictor," he said. "Why are you laughing?"

"Spent a lot of years in the Corp, Jonny," I said. "I know exactly what that is."

"What is it?"

"That's one big damn gun."

"There is a data crystal with the weapon, is there not?"

"Yeah the pedestal has one."

"Please bring it to me, friend Rictor," he said. "Perhaps we should leave the weapon until I see the databank."

"I don't think so," I said. "A gun never was any use locked up where you can't get to it. That sweet thing is coming with me."

Chapter 24

There were, perhaps thirty people gathered in the Rec Center, which is what we had started calling the large room at the center of Redoubt. It was a gathering point for people to just socialize. There were comfortable seats scattered around the large room.

Everyone was clustered around Peligios, who was strumming the guitar, and crooning a love song in the common language of all the planets except Earth.

He stopped, "Prophet! Come join us! We have taken the implant for your language. I would love to hear something from your world. Would you do us the honor?"

I smiled. I hadn't played for so many years. The night at the campfire had made me long for the days when I would sit and play for Jeanie. I stepped to where Peligios held the Cantumoor, I couldn't get used to that. It was a seven string not-guitar.

"What would you like to hear?"

"Your people liked the ballad you sang quite well," he said. "One of them was kind enough to translate it for me after. Do you know any love songs?"

"A couple," I said. "Here's one of unrequited love. I heard it in the '90's the first time."

I began playing a tune that brought me back to thoughts of Jeanie. Close to eighty years and I couldn't forget her.

Chris Isaak had done it better but I did my best with Wicked Game. I closed my eyes and just lost myself in the song. I could see Jeanie sitting under the dogwood tree in the woods, where I had asked for her hand. Her brilliant smile when I had asked that question. We had made love under that tree, and never parted from one another unless absolutely necessary. Her loss would haunt me for the rest of my life. A much longer life than I had intended when I joined the Corp.

When I finished I opened my eyes. Everyone was silent.

"That is a song I will have to play, Prophet. It is haunting."

"You have no idea," I muttered. "How about something a little less maudlin? I do know some fun stuff. CW McCall, Ray Stevens. I know some gunfighter ballads from Marty Robbins."

"Gunfighter?" he asked.

"Back a few hundred years ago, the western part of the United States was being explored. The law was scarce, and a man had to carry his own law with him. They used to say God made all men but Sam Colt made all men equal."

"By all means," Peligios said. "Sing some of these gunfighter ballads."

"Okay," I nodded. "Marty Robbins was a master of the gunfighter ballad. Let's start with 'Big Iron'. Always liked that one. Then maybe 'Utah Carol'."

I spent several hours in the Rec Center and the group grew quickly, as we passed the guitar back and forth singing songs of love, battle, and laughter. I sang "Ring of Fire" by Johnny Cash, which seemed fitting after I had lived that one when I fell into a burning ring of fire. I sang more of Johnny Horton, who was one of my favorites. I didn't do them all justice but I did my best. I listened to Peligios singing several songs. Most of what I heard were songs of loss.

These people had spent their whole lives losing. Back home there were decades where the common American suffered no loss. The same could be said of many countries. Here, they lost people to the Kresh on a regular basis. It was a part of their culture. It is why they were so eager to join. Hope that they could, perhaps, prevent some of that loss was something they never expected.

I know how slim our chances were of true success, and I think they did as well. But they still came. They learned fast because they believed in what they could see. It was less than three weeks from the arrival of the volunteers from Hollisab, which was one thirty two on our map that we left again for another run. We went in two directions this time. I sent First Guard Squad East to a village we were watching with the drones. Fifty-four looked promising. I took Third Squad and headed west toward another promising village, number eighty-eight. Weriona's squad numbered nine members, and this would be their first recruitment run.

I had seen Weriona talking with Huynini a few hours before we were set to go. I didn't listen in even though I could have. I think Weriona was asking tips from the more experienced Squad Leader. This was something I would encourage, wholeheartedly. This wasn't a contest.

Chapter 25

"They just hit the village," Weriona whispered.

"Looks that way," I said. "If Daras manages to get past them without being detected, we'll leave them be. I don't want a group that size disappearing here."

"We could take them," she said.

"Yeah, we could," I answered. "But no need to. They hit the village for supplies. They didn't take any people."

"Daras is hiding in that copse of trees," she said. "They are going to pass within a few feet."

I sighed, "Looks that way. Get formed up on me. V formation. If they catch him we'll hit 'em"

"Crodos, the god of chance, is not on our side today, Prophet."

"Indeed."

Daras was pulled from the copse by the leader of the party of close to a hundred Kresh. That leader was a Kresh'Sor'An, what I had known as a Wraith. I wasn't worried that I couldn't take the Wraith. I was worried Daras would be lost before I could.

"I will try a peaceful solution, first, Squad Leader. But gather your focus and prepare for a charge. Follow me."

I stood and strode down into the valley below where the Wraith was looking at Daras, and examining the clothing. Combat armor was not the normal dress worn by the Humans in the villages.

"Kresh'Sor'An," I said. "I would appreciate it if you would release my man. We are not here to fight, but we will if you choose that option."

The Wraith chuckled. Well, I think it was a chuckle, "Kill them. I will keep this one."

"You are making a mistake," I said. "But it is yours to make. Go."

The world slowed to a crawl, and I was running forward, swords in hand. My left sword shot like a bullet to bury itself in the chest of the Wraith. I was afraid to use disks. They might hit Daras The spasm of the Wraiths muscles sent Daras flying back to the side.

We hit the mob of Kresh as they charged at us. I heard a grunt behind me as Pol took a hit. A quick glance back showed a gash on his arm that had opened by one of the soldiers. Not life threatening, it would heal. I turned back to the job at hand, and led my Guards into the packed ranks of Kresh.

It was over fairly quickly as these things tend to be. Skirmishes were nothing like the hours spent in Kansas while we fought.

"I am sorry, Prophet," Daras was standing before me.

"Not your fault, Daras. Crodos wasn't with us today."

"Yes Sir."

Daras joined the others.

My head spun to the right as more Kresh came from the trees. Weriona's swords flamed.

"Hold!" I ordered. "These are noncombatants."

"They are witnesses," she said.

"We don't kill noncombatants," I said, placing my hand on her arm. "Crodos truly isn't with us today."

I looked to the females and small Kresh that clustered near the tree line. I pointed to the Wraith.

"He chose this, we did not," I said. "Gather the supplies you need and go."

In less than thirty minutes the Kresh were gone.

"I fear we may regret this," Weriona said. "It would not feel right to kill the young but they have seen us now."

"It was bound to get out sometime. We have to be more careful from here on out. They will be looking for us now. Shall we go see if we can get some more recruits? Then we need to burn these."

"Yes Sir," she answered. "Okay boys and girls, let's head to the village."

Weriona recruited thirty-two people after they saw what we had done to the band of Kresh. One of the couples were in their sixties. Weriona had said that the process would bring them back to a younger state, and Gharan had convinced his wife, Sylanna, to join us. The trip would be hard for them but the benefit could be worth the risk.

We moved back toward redoubt at a very leisurely pace after we cleaned up the mess where the Kresh had died.

Chapter 26

"Come, Prophet," Weriona said. "There is something you might wish to see."

I followed her to the left of the slow moving column of recruits.

"It is a Kilnyeri, Prophet," she said. "They seem to be the only creatures unafraid of us."

"I know," I answered. "We saw one on the first trip to Redoubt. I've never seen anything like them."

We peeked around a tree into a clearing with a small pool of water in the center.

"This Kilnyeri is very old," she said as we watched her move stiffly toward the pool. Seven tiny pieces of fluff followed closely behind.

"That is the cutest thing I ever saw," I said. "Amazing what they can do when riled up."

"Ruud has told us of the Kilnyeri you saw. That is why I thought you may like to see this one."

The Kilnyeri's head came up, quickly. Other shapes entered the clearing.

"That's odd," I said. "Most of the critters have already beat feet."

These resembled wolves in shape but the head was more akin to an alligator.

"Dhragathas," she said. "They run in packs. These must have been trailing the Kilnyeri and refused to give in to their sensing of Soul-guards."

"Who knows?" I returned. "I guess I can't expect the same reaction from critters here as we get on Earth. They should've run. I heard that a Kilnyeri can do some serious damage in a very short time when..."

We both saw the other Dhragathas come from the other side of the clearing.

"That could be bad," Weriona said. "She can't fight both groups at the same time. She will attack the largest group in the hopes that, at least some of her young escape. You will see. Kilnyeri are very smart. I'm afraid she is too old to succeed."

I sighed.

The dhragathas charged and, sure enough, the Kilnyeri launched herself into the group of seven. That left four charging in at the tiny fluffs.

The world slowed to a crawl as a rooster tail of dirt and grass shot from behind me. The dhragathas were less than a foot from the baby Kilnyeri when I intercepted them. The first two were slammed to the ground with a crack as their spines were crushed. Then I seized the other two by the necks from behind.

Glancing toward the Kilnyeri, I could tell she was nowhere near as fast as the young one I had seen before. Yet there were already three dead dhragathas. She seized one of the remaining four by the throat but the two behind her were too close. I spun and squeezed hard enough to kill both of the dhragathas I held. Then I threw the first one. Continuing the spin I threw the second one. The hand freed by throwing the first already held one of my swords, which shot across the space between the group and me, right behind the bodies of the dhragathas.

The first dhragatha impacted one of those behind the Kilnyeri. The other hit the second. They hit with enough force to send all four bodies tumbling across the clearing. My sword hit like a giant bullet through the chest of the only living dhragatha. It was inches from clamping those huge jaws onto the Kilnyeri. The sword exploded from the back of the dhragatha to continue across the clearing.

It seemed dhragathas aren't as tough as Kresh. I watched as it disappeared into the forest.

"Shit," I muttered.

The Kilnyeri turned incredibly quickly to see me standing over the dead dhragathas. Her young were all there. She had blood dripping from her fangs and her claws were crimson. Not quite as cute as before, but to an Ex-Marine, Hell, she was magnificent.

I gave her a nod and a short bow. Then I turned and walked away. I almost expected to feel the Kilnyeri slam into my back but she didn't attack.

"Only you would save the life of a Kilnyeri," Weriona said, shaking her head.

"Didn't like her odds," I said. "Thought I'd even em up a little. Besides, that sneaky shit, trying to kill her babies, bugs me."

She chuckled, still shaking her head, "Don't expect me to go look for that sword. It's probably a mile away."

I grinned, "I wonder if I shouldn't make it a training exercise."

She looked at me with one eye raised. I had a flashback to a few of the looks from Prada.

"Probably shouldn't push my luck," I muttered. "Get stabbed in my sleep or somethin'. Why I even let women into the new Guard, I don't know."

I was still grumbling when I entered the camp that the group had set up an hour and a half later. Weriona gave me that look again and I pointed at the second hilt jutting from the scabbard. She smiled and went back to trimming the meat in front of her. The blade was crimson with the blood of whatever pour creature she was cutting up and she looked distinctly like the Kilnyeri earlier.

"Crazy-assed women," I muttered and continued across the camp.

Chapter 27

"Olnyaq is definitely my favorite, so far," I said. "It has a little wild taste but it tastes a lot like pork. I love pork. God I miss bacon. I bet there's some bacon in an olnyaq, somewhere."

"What is bacon?"

"Thin slices of some of the fat parts of a pig. It is cured somehow."

"Ah," Trevos, a member of Third Squad, returned. "You mean salamor. It is too complicated to cure it on the trail, but when we get some olnyaq into the Redoubt, I know how to cure it."

"Oh my," I replied with my mouth watering. "We have to make gettin' some livestock in one of our priorities."

There was a commotion from the eastern edge of the camp as people scattered. I watched as the Kilnyeri from several days ago strode right into our camp, looking from side to side. She showed no fear and, right behind her, were seven little pieces of fluff the size of softballs.

I stayed seated as the Kilnyeri approached. She came within about three feet of me, and settled on her haunches. She looked me in the eye and cocked her head to the side. I remembered a dog my sister used to have. He was the smartest dog I had ever come across. He used to look at me like that.

I looked at my plate with a generous slab of olnyaq and a pile of the root that seemed commonplace around here that reminded me of a sweet potato. I slid my plate over to the Kilnyeri who examined it. Then she opened her hand-like paw with three inch razors and shredded the meat. She dragged small portions to her side along with pieces of not-potato. The seven fluff balls each had a pile and they dived in.

"Grab me another plate, Sami," I said.

The Kilnyeri had given all of the food to her young.

Sami was the guy who cooked the food. He had come in with the new recruits from the village. He said he had been the cook for a minor lord on Terajewid, one of the colony worlds.

He brought me a heaping plate of meat and not-potatoes. I took a knife he handed me and sliced the meat. I stabbed a piece and held it out to the Kilnyeri. She cocked her head to the side again and reached out with her clawed hand, taking the slice. I stabbed another slice and took a bite.

It was the damndest thing I had ever seen. I sat there for about twenty minutes with the whole camp staring in shock as I ate dinner with a Kilnyeri and her seven cubs.

After they finished stuffing themselves the Kilnyeri looked at me again with that cocked head and turned around. They filed back out of the camp as silently as they entered.

"How odd," I said. "Was that odd? That seemed odd."

"I have never seen anything quite like that, Prophet," Weriona answered. "I think, yes, that was odd."

Over the next hour, everyone finally settled down for the night. I kept getting disturbing looks from the recruits. And even a few from Third Squad. I tried to put it out of my mind as I drifted off to sleep, but I had dreams from my childhood about a stupid cat we used to have that always slept curled against my side. I woke up with a warm feeling against my side.

Weriona was sitting on a rock, staring at me. She motioned down at my side, and I looked to find seven softball-sized pieces of fluff nestled up against me.

"She came back during the night," she said motioning toward a form at the edge of the camp. "I was on watch. She sat there and watched until all seven crawled into your cloak. Then she laid down. She stopped breathing a few hours ago. I think you just became their new mother, Prophet."

I sighed as last night made a little more sense. Not any normal sense, but it made a sort of sense. She had seen me protect her young.

"Do you think she was showing me how to feed the things last night?"

"Maybe," she said. "Maybe she was seeing if you would."

"What am I going to do with seven fluffy balls of death?"

She laughed, "I have no idea, but it is certainly going to be fun to watch."

Chapter 28

"What are you doing with those?" Jonny asked as I crossed the beach from the tree line with a column of seven fluffy balls of death following me toward the rocks jutting out over the water.

"Seems I was charged with raisin' the little fluffs," I said. "Couldn't rightly decline after I stuck my nose in it."

"That should be an interesting story," he said.

I looked to the right as Weriona stepped out of the trees some distance down the beach. She had sent her scouts out before we had gotten to our destination.

"All clear," she reported on the coms.

"Alright, Jonny," I said. "Drain the tube and we'll get started. Thirty new recruits and six new dependents incoming. Please have them met at the bottom."

Six of the women in the party had youngsters on their hips. Both Gharan and Sylanna, our elder couple had made the trip well enough. I could see the exhaustion in their eyes, but they had done better than expected.

"Ladies and gentlemen," I said. "This spot behind me will begin to drain of water and we will slide down a tunnel to reach Redoubt. It is perfectly safe and has been used a great deal. You may even find it enjoyable. Those of you with youngsters, may be accompanied by a Guard to help manage your way down. You hold your child, they will hold you to keep you steady. The rest of you, place your arms out from you a small bit and let your palms steady you. If you feel you travel faster than you want, put pressure down with your hands. This will slow you a bit."

Everyone was looking at me with wide eyes.

"I didn't walk all this way to turn back now," Gharan said. It reminded me of my grandpa umpteen years ago. "Help me get up on that rock."

I grinned and offered my hand. Sylanna was right behind him with a grimace on her face.

"Too brave for his own good," she muttered.

"Nothin' to it Ma'am," I said. "We do it all the time. If it's any consolation, I have to do it with seven little fluffy balls of death in my arms."

She looked down at the Kilnyeri clustered at my feet and grinned. "Sure wouldn't want to do that."

I nodded. Gharan was looking into the hole.

"As you slide down watch the outside and you may see some of the technology the others have told you about. They will light your way down from outside of the tube."

Gharan grunted and sat on the edge of the rock, "Just slide into the hole, I guess."

He scooted forward and slid forward into the chute. Then he slid forward and around the first bend. I'm pretty sure I heard a version of "WOOOHOO!" in the local language about three turns of the spiral down. Sylanna shook her head and sat on the rock where her husband had just launched from.

"Hmph..."

Then she was sliding into the hole.

After seeing the two elders go the rest went much quicker. I don't think they wanted to be upstaged by a couple of old farts.

Weriona jumped onto the rock and shook her head as she looked down at the Kilnyeri, "You will indeed be lucky if they don't shred your uniform."

"They'll probably love it," I said. "Kilnyeri aren't afraid of anything."

She chuckled, "We will see, Prophet."

I squatted down and held my cloak out, nudging the little ones toward it. They climbed into the pouch I made of the bottom of the cloak.

I shrugged and jumped into the hole. They didn't shred my whole uniform but the cloak was definitely a goner. And the pants, and the shirt. They didn't hurt my boots.

They were trying, unsuccessfully, to hide the grins as I gathered all seven hissing fluffy balls of death back up and returned them to my tattered cloak.

"I wouldn't bend over like that, Prophet," Weriona chuckled. "There are things that shouldn't be seen by the children."

"Thought it was a little drafty," I said. "Grab that last one for me."

"I'd rather shave my head with a dull blade," she said. "Perhaps we will just turn around."

"I see how it's gonna be."

I hissed back at the seventh Kilnyeri and pointed to the others in my cloak. It jerked just a bit and stiff walked over and joined them.

"Show them who is in charge," Weriona nodded.

I pointed at her and pointed toward the Rec Center. She was still laughing as she led the new recruits toward that gathering point.

I reached into my cloak and began petting the fluffy balls of death.

"This cannot end well," Jonny said.

"Well if you think that was fun, wait till I start bringin' the olnyaq down through the tunnel. I was told they have bacon in 'em. I'll be throwing a few into the tunnel at the soonest opportunity."

"Truly?"

"Oh yes, truly."

I swear I forget he is an AI when he lets out a sigh like an overworked teacher.

I headed in the opposite direction of the crowd of recruits. I was in need of some clothes before returning to the group.

"Friend Rictor?"

"Yes?"

"What is bacon?"

"Heaven on Earth, Jonny, Heaven on Earth."

Chapter 29

"How are you this fine morning, Beautiful?" I asked as I walked into the room. "Did you miss me?"

My hand slid gently along the graceful curve of her stock.

"Sometimes I worry about your sanity, Friend Rictor," Jonny said. "The weapon cannot respond to you."

"Ten thousand years old with at least ten different personalities and you worry about my sanity?"

"We do not understand what you are speaking of."

"Why, Jonny," I returned. "Did you just make a joke?"

"I have been studying Humans since coming into contact with you again, Friend Rictor. I had very little contact with the first Humans who came here. After they were gone I didn't have the chance for all this time. I find that I like this humor I see in you and the others. I am exploring it."

"It was good, Jonny. Subtle humor is some of the best," I said as my hand slid along the barrel of the weapon. "Isn't that right, Gorgeous?"

"There is no Gestalt in the weapon, Friend Rictor."

"Ah but there doesn't need to be, Jonny. She is a beautiful thing. Ten thousand or more years and no rust, no corrosion. Marilyn, here, can probably express herself quite well."

"Marilyn?"

"You're thinkin' I named her after Marilyn Monroe," I said. "Not true."

"There was a girl in Saigon," I continued. "She was gorgeous, Jonny. The one thing she wanted more than anything else was to be American. She spent a lot of time in the bars with the soldiers, did some things for money we'll not speak of. She wanted to be American so much she called herself Marilyn. I mean, what's more American than that?"

"Then she came in one evenin' and told her many admirers that she wouldn't be able to do the things she used to because she was pregnant and would have stop."

"Well, Jonny, some of those fellas didn't think she should stop what they came to her for and they tried to take what she used to offer by force. Hell, she beat the shit out of all three of those boys. Before the others in the bar could come for her in revenge, my boys surrounded her."

"I got a feelin' any weapon that was so feared that it had to be stored a couple thousand feet under an ocean is well deserving of that namesake."

"Friend Rictor?"

"Yeah?"

"Who is Marilyn Monroe?"

I sighed, "Never mind, buddy."

"Will you please not let that creature play with the weapon?"

One of the fluffy balls of death had crawled from my cloak and was climbing "Marilyn's" stock. I plucked the Kilnyeri from the gun and placed it on my shoulder where it quickly made itself comfortable against my neck.

"So, have you found out what she does?"

"It is a weapon based around portal technology. This much I can tell through examination. What the portals are connected to, I cannot say. The fact it was deemed too dangerous to be inside of this facility says it is something very powerful."

"So she might just be the right sort of thing for me," I said. "Maybe I should go fire it."

"I would prefer if you did not, Friend Rictor," he said. "What if it is connected to something too powerful on the other side?"

"How bad could it be?"

"Example: It is connected to a portal that opens on our system's star. Just opening that portal would more than likely destroy the one holding the weapon, the one the weapon is aimed at, the weapon itself, and have a strong likelihood of destroying the planet on which it is used."

"Gotta say that sounds bad," I said.

"There is a very small chance they would do something this foolhardy. There are two portals that seem to be set to open when the weapon is fired. Therefore, two sources of whatever damage the weapon would consider ammunition. It is unknown what those two sources are so we may never know what this weapon truly is."

"So, basically, I don't get to fire Marilyn."

"Exactly," he answered. "Furthermore, I think the weapon should be returned to the vault where we found it."

"A gun is useless when it is locked up where it can't be reached."

"I take that as a negative response to returning the weapon," he said. "Perhaps I can convince you to at least let me put it on a drone where it will not be inside of Redoubt?"

My hand slid once more across the stock and I let out a long sigh, "I guess I can handle that. At least long enough for you to figure out what she can do."

Chapter 30

"There ain't no sunshine when she's gone...." My voice carried across the room as I sang another song that reminded me of Jeanie. Bill Withers did it better but I still gave it a try.

My eyes closed and I lost myself for a few seconds in the song. Then I found myself looking into those beautiful blue eyes...No, they were green. Or were they blue? I couldn't remember. God, how could I forget?

My voice faltered and I sank into silence as I remembered her eyes as they pushed me out of the Delivery room. Her blue eyes closed for the last time and I remembered that feeling when they told me I was alone in this world.

"Prophet?"

"Sorry, Peligios," I said with a hoarse voice. "That has to be a song for another day."

He nodded as he saw me wipe my hand across my eyes. How could I have forgotten something like that? Even for an instant.

He nodded and took the not-guitar as I handed it to him. I stood and nodded to the crowd of listeners before heading for the exit.

As I neared the door that led to the Exercise Yard I heard a voice, "Why did you stop singing, Prophet?"

It was one of the older children, a girl of about seven years.

"Linandera," I said and squatted down to look her in the eyes. "I lost someone very dear to me a long time ago. I had to watch, helplessly as she was taken."

"Is that why you saved us from the Masters?"

"Part of it," I said, placing my hand on her shoulder. "I won't stand there helpless anymore. Not when I can do something about it."

"Momma says you have given all of us a future that could never have been dreamed of until now. If you want, I will be your friend. Then you don't have to be sad because your other friend left."

I swallowed.

"Thank you, Linandera," I said. "Perhaps."

She grinned and ran back to her mother, Tinastella. She was looking at me with a sad expression. With her Soulstream knotted, I knew she had heard the exchange. I nodded to her and left the room.

I made my way to the barracks. We'd set up an area like I had been living in for eighty years. There were bunks just like I had at Parris Island when I first joined the Corp. We could have set up private quarters for everyone but this was part of the building of a brotherhood of sorts. Once you tied your knot and finished your basic training with Salker Ruud, there were private quarters provided. My quarters were located right in the center of it all. As soon as I entered, I was bombarded by seven fluffy balls of death.

They had grown more accustom to the redoubt, and didn't have to follow me everywhere. Although they would if I let them. After catching Sadyuni playing with one of them, I decided to let them grow more comfortable with Humans before too much interaction with those not powered by a Soulguard knot. Most days, I would take one or two out with me to gain that experience.

I probably didn't have to worry about it. The beasts were quite smart, and they sensed the smaller amount of power flowing through the folks who hadn't tied their knots. I could see a deliberate gentleness from them toward those that hadn't. Which didn't help me, personally, one whit as they all pounced.

"I know, I know, you little fluffy turds," I muttered. "Time to go out and play."

They heard the word "out" and they stopped chewing on various parts of me to climb to their "travel" positions. Did I say they were smart? I mean very smart. Four of them piled into the hood of my cloak and the others perched on my shoulders, clinging to the padding of the shirt Jonny had made for me. It had thick areas for them to grasp.

Stepping back out the door, we retraced my steps through the barracks and around the hub of the facility toward the area Jonny used to have livestock back when he was first created. He had kept the enormous cavern full of vegetation which added to the oxygen levels for the redoubt. He had been able to cut back on the Carbon Dioxide production after moving more Humans down into Redoubt.

The skill of the ancients amazed me but I had no doubt of their Humanity. We keep doing the wrong things as a race on Earth and I could see the same from the ancients. Create a race of creatures that overthrow you and enslave you. That's what Earth would probably do if they had the technology to pull it off.

As I entered the massive cavern the kids were chirping loudly and launched themselves from my shoulders into the vegetation. I sat down on a rock to watch them play.

It truly disturbed me that I had forgotten the color of her eyes for that short moment. How could I have done that? It was so long ago, but I had never forgotten. Even when I tried to bury myself in the early years. I had buried myself in alcohol, women, and war. But I could never stop remembering.

Here I stood, decades later, never wishing to forget and finding my memories slipping. It was more terrifying to me than anything I had ever faced.

Chapter 31

The beach was a welcome sight. I knew this was necessary to our success, but sometimes these recruiting patrols were rough. Those people in number one eighty-two on our map, now known as Taro since we had been through, were filled with a fear so ingrained we only came back with five volunteers.

"Long distance for so few," I said.

"Very true, Friend Rictor," Jonny answered. "I have good news, though."

"What's that?"

"We should have the Gate ready to test in a few weeks. Friend Relki loves to learn, and she is almost ready to try to open the Gate. There are a few more simple lessons and we can have a trial."

"That's great news, Jonny!"

The scouts stepped from the tree line and signaled to Huynini.

"All is clear, my Prophet," she grinned.

"Good job, people," I said. "What say we get back home? Jonny, drain the tunnel if you please."

Huynini jumped to the rock, "If you will please join me, I will instruct you on what is about to happen."

"Friend Rictor," Jonny said, "I must ask if you have..."

Static filled the coms and I peered down the tunnel, "Jonny?"

Huynini slammed into my back and I tumbled into the tunnel.

The static was suddenly gone as I heard her voice on the com, "It seems the Prophet has decided to greet you at the bottom, my friends. Welcome to Redoubt."

I was still laughing as I slid through the airlock and across the slick floor at the receiving end of the slide.

"That was unfair, Jonny," I said. "Underhanded and sneaky. I like it! Prada would be proud."

"Who is Prada, friend Rictor?" he asked. "And the one to blame for this is standing atop that rock on the surface, barely able to speak through the smile in her face."

"I figured it would be one of those conniving women," I said. "But you're supposed to have my back."

"You seemed happy about my experiments with humor..."

"Oh, you're gonna play that card. I see how it is."

I got to my feet and turned to greet the newcomers as they slid into sight. This was the first time I was on the receiving end of the slide to see the expressions of those who used it for the first time.

"Glad you have the portal almost ready, Jonny," I said, seeing the wide eyes of the first young man to slide into view. "I never really took into account the initial entry has on a lot of people."

"It is true," he said. "It seems to be quite startling to most of them."

"It's funny that something like this is so scary and people find teleporting through friggin' wormholes normal. Frankly, the damn gates make me nervous."

First Squad slid into view, one by one with barely concealed grins. The First guard, herself didn't even try to disguise her smile.

"If you will follow me," she said to the five new recruits, "We will get you introduced to the others."

She glanced at me as she led them toward the Rec Center with a huge grin. I was barely restraining my own laughter so it was hard to keep the stern look on my face. There wasn't the slightest hint of remorse that I could see in the tiny woman.

"She has changed so much from the girl who was thrown into our village with six others, five years ago," Salker said from behind me.

"I don't doubt it."

"You have no idea, Prophet," he said. "She comes from Therrasin, a high population colony. They have hundreds of millions of people there. Some will go their whole life without seeing any of the Masters. They go through life assured of a future... unless they are taken by the Masters."

"They are given a taste of a life where they can look to the future," he continued. "It makes it much harder on those that are taken. We all have lived with the knowledge that when a person is taken, they never get to go back home. Their future is now with the Masters. The high population means less chance of being taken, and thus a harder reaction when it occurs."

"I could see that," I said.

"She arrived, completely devastated. It was hard to even bring her around to the idea she still had a life. A young man made it his priority to show her. He succeeded for the most part and they were married within the first year."

"Sadyuni's father?"

He nodded, "The Masters took him about a year ago and Huynini was as close to hopelessness as I had ever seen her. Odasa, her heart-sister helped with Sadyuni for a time until she began to seek her way back to us. Then the Masters came again and took us."

"Rough way to go," I muttered.

"I am convinced she would have taken her own life if you had not walked right out of nowhere with a new dream for all of us. You gave her this chance to become so much more than the victim she had been. Now she is a warrior, and I guarantee she will die before a Kresh ever 'takes' her anywhere."

Chapter 32

Striding through the forest to the west of Redoubt, I glanced behind me at the seven fluffy balls of death. They had grown quickly to basketball-sized fuzzy menaces. I stopped at the base of a huge tree and climbed upward.

"Come on," I said.

They swarmed up the tree.

"Ouch...ouch... There's a whole other side of the tree," I muttered. "No... you have to crawl up me."

I pointed out a limb with dense foliage, and they crawled out on the limb. We crouched there for some time before hearing noise from further inside the trees.

I held my hand out, palm down and the Kilnyeri all seemed to tense up as they prepared to spring. A few moments later their prey came into view. Three forms walked along the path. As they passed by the tree where we crouched, I turned my hand palm up. The Kilnyeri looked like fuzzy cannonballs as they slammed into the backs of three members of Third Squad. Two hit Firennia, two hit Pol, and the other three tackled Weriona. All seven were out of reach of the Guards before their enhanced reflexes could let them catch the attackers.

"Those little monsters are fast," Weriona said as she regained her feet.

I landed lightly on the trail, "That, they are."

"They hit hard," Pol said.

Firennia, by far the smallest of the three had been knocked completely off the trail.

"That was uncalled for, Prophet," she said. "What did we do to deserve being bombarded by the fluffy balls of death?"

"Just wait," I said. "The rest of Third squad are next."

There was a commotion from deeper in the forest and a few yelps.

Weriona was grinning widely, "I hope they hit Sandorl extra hard. He needs some waking up. Always last in every exercise we do."

"There's always somebody who has to be last," Pol said.

"It shouldn't be consistently the same one," she said.

"She's right, there," I said.

"We will get him straightened out, Prophet," Weriona returned.

There was another commotion, and some yells as the Kilnyeri hit another three-man team. The squad would be broken down in three-man teams. Those teams would be listed from one to eight all under the command of Squad Leader Weriona who was part of a three-man team as well. Totaling twenty-seven people per Squad. Third squad had fifteen people so far and the ranks were growing all the time.

Redoubt held five hundred and eighty-two people by this time, and we had been to half of the one hundred and ninety villages that were nestled inside of the triangle of three Kresh Enclaves. Sixty of those people had successfully finished Ruud's training, and had been added to the squadrons.

Seven streaks came out of the forest to cluster at my feet.

"You did great," I mumbled to them as I squatted down to pet them all.

"I swear, it is disturbing to see you playing with one of the most fearsome creatures that live on Fhlo'Saa'Gellis," Weriona said.

Three of the Kilnyeri ran to her, and she petted them too.

"Even more disturbing when I do it myself," she muttered.

Chapter 33

When I came around the corner into the training area, it was to a strange sight. Thirty recruits and guards were scattered throughout the large area practicing with weapons. That wasn't the truly strange part.

"Is that a scythe?" I asked as I stepped up to stand beside Salker.

"Indeed it is, Prophet."

"An axe?"

"Assuredly," he returned as we looked at Gers. He looked like a Viking from Norse mythology as he spun around with the huge double bladed axe. "He started training with a double blade woodcutter's axe."

"Each person here has a skill with a tool that they are proficient with. Gers chopped wood for our village for the last four years. He knows the use of an axe. Therefore, I will use that proficiency to teach him how that axe can be a magnificent weapon."

"We played with some of this as Soul-guards, but the swords were designed to work together as a unit."

"This I know, Prophet," he nodded with a smile. "But we both know that the man or woman is the weapon, the sword or the axe is the tool. A warrior should be able to use anything as a tool of war. You see Yarnust Krole, the cutter of hay? He will be able to harvest a crop of death with that scythe. He has swung that tool for ten years, Prophet. It is comfortable in his hand and he is familiar with every aspect of using that tool. It can be a devastating weapon in the hands of one who is familiar with it."

"I'm not complaining," I said. "I figured out from the beginning that things would be different here on Fhlo'Saa'Gellis."

"In Strykland, my former home on Parlais, we train from the day we can hold a knife. It is what every person on our planet is very good at. There are farmers and there are servants, each carries a blade and all are paid for their services. There are people who prefer not to be on the front lines as we fight our hostile neighbors. They choose these professions because they can make their living doing these things. Every job they do is done while striving at their honorable profession. But each one of them have spent many years in training."

"I understand your proficiency with weapons a bit more," I said.

We watched in silence for a moment.

"When a Parlaisian is born, he or she is taken down into the Depths," he said. "There we stay until we turn fifteen years in age. The Depths are a secret catacomb under the fortress, where we stay hidden from the Masters. There we receive education from the most knowledgeable of our people."

"Seems a little harsh," I said.

"Not really," he answered. "It is the only time in a Parlaisian's life when he is truly safe. I have fond memories of my time in the Depths. We are not exiled, our families spend a great deal of time with us. We are trained with weapons and words. Tactics and Logistics. Some are better suited to join the Workers, some the Warriors, both honorable professions. There are many professions from cook to providers of pleasure, farmers and fishermen."

"I see," I returned. "Not as harsh as my first impression. But it should not be necessary to hide our children from someone who could take them at any moment. What the Kresh have done well and truly pisses me off."

"I can see your world in my head, and it amazes me that you can have so much freedom. You speak of great universities where the young can come and learn anything they wish. Right out in the open and unguarded."

"It left us unprepared for what came later," I said. "We lost over a million people in the advance attacks by the Kresh before Second Kansas. Colin swore he wished to see each and every human with a Soulguard knot. Yet we were restricted by the oaths to the Soulguard. I wasn't so sure about it until I saw what they did in New York. Several thousand Kresh just erupted in the middle of a city packed with eight million people. It was a slaughter."

"It is hard to see that many losses in skirmishes in my head. So many people packed together in a single city is truly amazing."

"There are cities overseas with more," I said. "The planet has a population of over six billion."

He just shook his head in wonder, "I can see where you would look at the Depths as a harsh thing."

"Sounds pretty smart," I said. "In all honesty, it is better solution than many of the worlds have come up with. Everyone is educated and everyone knows how to defend themselves. Here we do the same thing, we provide the avenue where they can defend themselves. Only this is defense from the Masters."

"That it is, Prophet."

Chapter 34

"What would you think about sending out your drones to begin building another facility like this one?" I asked.

"That would be a major undertaking, friend Rictor."

"I know, but I want you to think on it a little, Jonny," I said as I packed the duffle I would take out on this recruitment run.

"You always pack much more tissue than you need, friend Rictor," he said as I stuck another roll in my pack.

"Someone always forgets their toilet paper," I returned. "Never fails with new recruits. First has six new members this time."

"You should take the sonic cleaners, friend Rictor."

"That's tech that gets the owner killed immediately," I said. "Swords and combat armor are curiosities. That is forbidden tech. We always run the chance of capture. Guards are no match for a Kresh'Farrara'Ti. They run up against something like that, I don't want them killed because of tech."

"What happens if one of them is encountered?"

"It gets ugly, Jonny," I said. "I don't even know how successful I would be with one like that. I saw one in Montana but I didn't see it fight. I have seen one of their Ma'Nar and they're tough. They have shields and I don't know what it would take to get through them."

"How was it defeated?"

"Rash'Tor'Ri killed it. He can manipulate their shields as easily as he can his own. He just rips through them and kills anything in his path."

"Rash'Tor'Ri seems to be quite formidable, friend Rictor."

"That, he is," I returned. "Is First Squad ready?"

"Yes they are forming up in the receiving bay."

"Good," I said, placing the last item in my pack. "This should be a minor run. Will the gate be ready to test in a couple of weeks?"

"We can test in less time," he answered. "We will certainly be ready to test the gate when you get back."

"That's going to make things so much easier. I still have a hard time with the idea of people walking through a wormhole without fear and being terrified of the slide."

"There are a great many things I don't understand about humans, friend Rictor. This is one that I do. The portals have been a part of their lives. Holes in the ocean to slide down under the water?"

"Yeah, I guess they don't see that every day," I chuckled.

***

"Bollinger," Huynini said, "Take your team ahead and get us an olnyaq or two to give them when we get there."

"Ma'am," he nodded and three of them peeled off from the group to disappear into the forest ahead of us.

Bollinger was relatively new to First Squad, but he had become quite good. He made Team Leader very quickly. He was followed by Marrin, a stocky light skinned woman from Terajewid. She had come from the same village as

Sami and they had been taken from Terajewid at the same time. The third member of their team was Tolver, small, dark haired, and dark skinned. He was from Lastel, a low population colony. His world was violent to the extreme and he bore many scars from the struggle to stay alive. The Kresh had a large arena like the Romans used to use and they liked to use Lastelians for their entertainment.

Tolver wasn't leadership material, but he was probably the best fighter in the Squad. I'd known Marines like him. If you want something killed, you point them at it and let them go. I had spent some time in the same state of mind after I joined the Marines.

"Shall we camp for the night, Prophet?" Huynini asked. "It is late and I would rather approach them in the morning."

"Sounds good," I nodded.

"Rolan," she ordered, "Water. Tar'Weelus, wood. Jaharis, the Prophet's quarters."

"Prophet's quarters?" I asked.

"Shhh."

"Did you shhh me?" I asked. "I think she shhh'd me."

She pointed at me with that one eyebrow raised, "No arguments."

Yarnust Krole, third of Jaharis's team had pulled a bundle of canvas from his pack. They made short work setting up a very nice tent.

"I don't need a tent..."

"This has been discussed at the highest levels. There is no use in arguing about it."

I made my way to the tent with my head shaking.

"Thought I was the highest level," I muttered.

"What was that?" she asked.

"Nothing," I said and pulled the entry flap aside to look in the tent."

It was a pretty large tent for one person. Probably fifteen feet long by ten wide. It would make a good command tent later on.

Chapter 35

Thunder woke me and I heard fat drops of rain hitting the top of the tent. I peeked out at the camp to find everyone awake. The lightning from that thunder had been close.

"Get in here," I said.

"It was made for you, my Prophet," Huynini said.

"Today it is for you," I said with a grin. "Tomorrow I'll take ownership of the tent."

None of them argued further but I could see the grin on Jaharis' face. He had been through many storms at sea I would imagine.

"I'll take the watch," I said. "Jonny said it looked like there may be storms moving through the area."

Pulling a poncho that he had made for me from my bag I grinned, "Brought this, just in case."

It was crowded, but they all fit in the tent.

Jaharis returned to the door flap, "I will also take watch."

It was common for us to use two at a time on watch and he didn't have the ingrained fear of storms the others were feeling.

I threw the poncho to him.

"You should keep this, Prophet."

"I have other ways," I said and stepped out into the now pouring rain.

The rain seemed to stop about two feet above my head and run off to the sides.

Jaharis grinned, "I would love to be able to do that."

"Once we start the personal shields you may be able to," I said. "Colin showed us how to do that when we were Guards. The Guard's shield is much weaker than a Mage shield and may not stop a Wraith. But it will definitely be good enough to keep rain off your head."

I took a seat on a rock beside the fire that was beginning to fade and raised another shield. It took a moment to get it made because I had to make a chimney top of sorts. I tried a few times but ended up with a tube that pointed up and turned a sharp right at the top to keep the rain from entering the hole. It worked.

Jaharis joined me under the canopy shield and I turned my "Umbrella" off.

"So how did you end up where the Kresh could pick you up, Jaharis?"

"As you know, my people took to the sea," he said. "We live in floating Enclaves. My Enclave was called Dassana, named after the daughter of Dianae, Mistress of the Deeps and Goddess of Death."

I nodded.

"We were attacked by a rival Enclave, Kilmar. We held them off, but they took some captives. My ship and five others pursued. We caught them and fought, ship to ship. We defeated them, and retrieved our people. Unfortunately, my ship took damage and we lagged behind as the others returned to Dassana."

"A great mother of a storm hit us and the Arkfyre went down. I managed to climb onto some of the wreckage and had almost accepted that I would be seeing Dianae soon. I washed ashore, barely able to move and the Kresh picked me up."

"I should have ended my life but I am glad I did not," he said.

"I'm glad, too, Jaharis. Perhaps we can get you back to Krongis someday to rejoin your people."

"No one ever returns after the Masters take them."

"No one ever killed the Masters with their bare hands, either."

"Very true," he grinned. "It would truly be a wonder to stand on the decks of Dassana again."

I stood up, "Going to do a circle of the camp. Shouldn't be far enough out for the shield to go down but I'd put on the poncho just in case."

He removed his twin swords from their scabbards and pulled the poncho over his head. The swords lay within easy reach of his hands.

I opened the umbrella shield and stepped out of the canopy shield. Taking my time, I circled the camp several times. If it wasn't raining, I would have gone to circle the village ahead of us. I didn't want to drop the canopy over the fire and leave Jaharis in the rain.

It was still raining when the dawn broke, but not as hard. The lightning had passed through hours back. Huynini was the first to exit the tent. As she looked out at the pouring rain, she shook her head.

"Someone had too many lokasa beans," she said as she stepped out into the downpour.

I waved her over to the fire. Looking at the shield canopy over the fire in wonder, she joined us.

"You never cease to amaze me, my Prophet," she said. "First night with the tent and you give it to us."

"It was plenty dry under the canopy," I said.

"I see," she said, "You didn't share a tent with twelve others, of which at least one ate too many lokasa beans."

"I saw Bollinger eating those yesterday," I grinned.

"Not surprising."

Chapter 36

"We want nothing to do with you," Boligg, the Overman of Varden, assured Huynini. "Your presence here is not welcome."

"You have not heard what we have to offer," she returned.

"We have heard of your Prophet and his claims," he continued. "We have heard from the Masters about what will happen if we have any contact with you. We want you to leave, immediately!"

"Then we leave," I said. "Pull the squad out and head home, First."

"But..."

Her head snapped to the right, just like mine and every other person at the edge of Varden.

"No," I heard the despair in Boligg's voice.

When I first arrived, my senses were bombarded by that sense of wrongness we had all associated with the Kresh. Fhlo'Saa'Gellis had millions of them. Since that time I had begun to discern the difference between that "background noise" and the presence of many Kresh closing on our position. I probably wouldn't notice ten or twenty but what we sensed approaching wasn't a small party.

"Get your people inside," I said. I grabbed his shoulder, "I am truly sorry, Boligg. We would have left you be as you asked. A person has to choose his own way in a world of free men and women."

He sighed but acknowledged what I said with a nod, "Yet the choice is made for us, once again."

"I am going to remove the force that's coming," I said as flames began to roll across my body. "The choice after that is done is your own."

"First squad! Form on the Prophet!" Huynini ordered. "Formation Bravo!"

Bravo would be a good choice. It was a wedge, much like what we used with Colin as the tip. Only the formation was made by the triangle formations of the three man teams. There was always one on the inside that was a rear guard, as well as a man to step in if one of the wedge falls. One three man team is inside the wedge to do the same.

I could see them across the open plain to the west. The enhanced vision from my body's extra energies from the Source allowed me to discern the shapes of three larger forms in the rear.

"Wraiths," I said. "Rear of the formation. I'll take care of them. You don't want to tangle with those. We're going straight through the horde to them."

"Yes, my Prophet."

I launched myself forward with First squad holding a tight formation to my sides.

"Spread!" Huynini ordered and the formation spread out to have about five feet between each person.

Grinning, I pointed us at the center of the Kresh that had seen us and poured across the plain. This was First Squad's first true test against the Kresh in numbers and Huynini's people were doing everything by the book.

We hit the center of the incoming horde and cut through the soldiers at a rate that shocked them. They expected to roll us underfoot. We were halfway to the Wraiths before they even realized we weren't the humans they expected.

I began Pulling from the Source and had to concentrate to keep myself in the formation while my body vibrated with power.

"First! Take point!"

Huynini's team slipped right into position behind me and the wedge was formed on her. I leaped into the air and the world slowed to a crawl. The Kresh had not expected Humans who could fight them and win. They certainly didn't expect this.

My body's ability to store so much of the Source made this attack devastating. I Pulled hard and sent disks flying from my launchers that slammed into two of the Wraiths. The third got the Soullance with all of the power I had been storing up.

It was overkill but I needed to let the power go before I stored too much. I wasn't feeling any of the burn yet and hadn't found where the limits of that particular skill were located yet. Soon I would have to explore that.

The Kresh roared in unison.

"You seem to have made them angry," Bollinger said with a grin as I landed just behind the formation where he and his fire team held the rear.

"Just a little," I laughed. "First! Keep moving. Sweep across 'em and return. Don't let 'em bog you down in one spot."

"Yes, my Prophet."

"Not a Prophet."

"Of course," she returned and the formation turned to the left to sweep across the horde of Kresh. "A Prophet would say exactly that."

With a sigh, I raised my launchers higher above the heads of the Guards in front of me and began lofting disks into the Kresh soldiers. A couple of sweeps left piles of Kresh in smoking ruin.

"Perhaps we should have stayed back at the village and just sent him," Jaharis said.

"Next time we should start with the Prophet and perhaps I would not have pieces of Kresh in my hair," Tar'Weelus, a large blonde woman from Yevinn'Tor added.

"I can get those out for you," Rolan, Third team leader, returned.

I had a flashback to a cave in Arkansas and a similar conversation between Andrea Prada and Ivan Jacobs. Laughing loudly, I launched my disks again into the mass of Kresh.

When all was said and done, we had seven Guards with injuries, most of which were already in the process of healing.

"Hold that cut together as best you can, Jaharis," I said. "It will leave less of a scar."

"Women love scars, Prophet."

Another flashback. Soldiers are soldiers, no matter what world they come from.

Chapter 37

"There were no survivors, Boligg," I said. "You still have a choice. We will leave you in peace."

"You know a group of Kresh that size does not just disappear! There is no choice. If we stay here, we will be destroyed!"

"Then come with us. You can join us as recruits, or you can come, and we will house you in Redoubt. Not everyone is able to do what these do."

I was pointing toward the members of First Squad as they were cleaning the evidence of the battle from the plain where we had fought a day earlier.

"I suppose we must."

"Then pack what supplies you need to make a two week journey. We can hunt meat but you may have the stores to save the trouble. If there is no one staying here, there is no use leaving behind the food. We can provide clothing and food in Redoubt, but if there is anything personal that you wish to take, bring it. Tell them to remember they will carry what they bring and it is a two week journey."

He nodded with a scowl on his face and returned to Varden. I could understand his ire. He didn't want to endanger his people and that was an admirable trait in a leader. But there comes a time when you must take risks. He was right in the fact that they really had no choice and I hated that fact. Due to my actions, they had to give up everything they knew. After they reached Redoubt, some of that ire may fade.

"My grandmother used to do that," Huynini said, standing beside me.

I looked in the direction she was staring. An older woman was sitting on a chair sewing small pieces of cloth together.

"Looks like she's making a quilt."

"Yes."

"Your grandmother liked to quilt?"

"She would sit on her porch and sew all day long," she said. "After a couple of weeks, she would take a stack of quilts to town and see the traders. She would buy any small cloth left over from the tailor and the rest would buy food and such for the family."

"We used to have some of the quilts Jeannie's mother had made before..."

She continued, filling the silent void my unfinished sentence left, "My mother hated sewing. Perhaps she did because she had to help Gran with the quilts. I rather enjoyed it, myself. Gran was such good company. She had stories she would tell us every night. When you are ready, you can tell us the story of the lady you lost."

"How did you know about that?"

"We are simple people, Prophet. Not blind. The songs of loss you have sung to us are not just songs to you. You stop when you almost start to talk about it. Only the loss of a loved one can hurt a person so."

"I look out at this world and I see loss everywhere," I said. "Not one person hasn't lost someone dear to them, and they go forward. Eighty years I've gone since losing them and I can't finish a sentence about her."

"That speaks to the character of a person. She must have been a spectacular woman," she said and walked away before I could say anything else.

"That she was," I muttered.

I could hear the loud voices inside the village as Boligg informed people of the choices left to them. There was a lot of anger in those voices. This was not going to be a pleasant trip back to Redoubt.

Shaking my head, I returned to the clearing where First Squad had piled the bodies of the Kresh. Frustrated by the reactions of the people of Varden, I began to Pull into myself.

For freedom to truly be freedom I had to accept the fact that some of these people wouldn't be fighters. So far we had brought volunteers to Redoubt. They were willing to fight and they tried to become Soulguards.

These would be different. They came because they had no better choices left to them. Perhaps a few of them would come around.

"We'll see," I muttered and released the Soulfire from inside me to engulf the huge pile of bodies. Regular flame would leave bones and such. Soulfire would destroy all evidence.

Chapter 38

"Jonny's going to love this," I said.

I was perched on the top of a bluff, looking down at our caravan. The villagers of Varden had brought everything. They had crafted makeshift carts to carry their belongings. Along with the ninety villagers, we had forty domestic olnyaq and twenty-eight creatures about the size of a horse but looked more like some sort of lizard based animal. They called them dolga. Also there were cages of birds a little bigger than a chicken.

"I could use some eggs and bacon," I said and turned to fade back into the tree line. There was a strong animosity toward me with these folks but it didn't seem to pass down to the others. I went out a little more often to hunt than I would normally have gone.

"Jonny is going to love what?" his voice was barely discernable through the static.

"You'll see," I answered. "When the drone gets close enough. You better have the Gate ready to use. Your bots get to herd all these critters back up if I have to throw them down the slide."

"Critters?" he asked. "That is a new word in your language. How am I supposed to use this awful language when you continue to make new words?"

"Keeps life interesting," I laughed.

"What did you do?" he asked as his drone closed the distance enough to see the caravan. "Did you bring the entire village?"

"As a matter of fact, we did," I answered. "There was an incident."

"Of course there was."

"I see how it's gonna be."

"Friend Rictor, you should see what has just occurred," he said.

The contact in my right eye flickered and I saw a view from Jonny's drone. The caravan had halted and started preparing their camp. The drone focused on a rock overhang above the small lake where they set up. A girl climbed the rock and tumbled off to fall in the deep water underneath with a scream.

Huynini was in the water before anyone else could even react and she retrieved the child. Boligg was at the water to meet her when she came out and held the crying girl to his chest.

"Good job, First," I said over the coms now that we had a drone to relay.

She looked to the sky when she heard me. Our coms work with Jonny's drones or sensors. We don't carry any sort of equipment other than the implant Jonny put in each of us.

She waved at the drone with a grin.

The rest of our trek back to Redoubt went smoothly. Boligg was a little less belligerent and that made me much happier. Some of the others didn't share that gratitude over their child being rescued and I wondered how they would do after joining those in Redoubt.

"Clear the beach!" ordered Huynini. First squad scattered as we neared the tree line next to the entrance.

"Okay, Jonny," I said. "Have you gotten the gate ready?"

"It has yet to be tested but I am certain it will work. It should be set to open on the beach in front of you."

"As soon as she gives the word, open it and we'll see if it works."

"Clear!"

Moments later the air in front of me shimmered and I felt that eerie feeling we had associated with Kresh invasion on my world.

Then the portal was fully formed, glowing with the multicolored fire of what I now knew was the Source channeled through the machinery.

"Let's see how it does," I said and stepped toward the gate.

A hand settled on my shoulder, "You are not the test."

Huynini strode past me and stepped into the glowing surface.

"First?" I asked on coms.

"The Gate works great," her voice replied. "Send them on."

"All right folks," I turned back to the crowd on the beach, "On the other side of this gate is Redoubt. You are welcome to make yourse..."

Something slammed into my back from the portal and I staggered forward. Then six other forms hit me and I tumbled over to the ground, laughing.

As I rolled on the beach with seven Kilnyeri chewing on my arms and legs, the rest of First squad steered the horrified villagers past us and into the portal.

"Are those Kilnyeri?" asked Torastey, one of the villagers.

"Yes," Bollinger sighed. "It's a long story which we'll tell you during the introduction process."

"I still wondered if what you had been telling me was true until this moment," he said. "That is something I would never have believed if I had not just seen it."

"Should have been there when the mother Kilnyeri decided he was going to finish raising her young."

"Truly?"

"Seriously, we will tell you all about it."

Torastey walked into the gate shaking his head in wonder.

Chapter 39

Four kids ran into the water to my right as I lounged on the rocks beside the entrance to Redoubt. Three others climbed past me and dived inside of the slide that led down to the facility with squeals that faded as they descended.

"Glad Tinastella thought of this, Jonny," I said.

"It seems the children needed to see the sky," he answered. "Some things I do understand, friend Rictor. When something one has known in your life is taken away, one longs for that to come back. The sky for these young humans is like that."

"One might think you were talkin' about the presence of people in a certain facility."

"One might, friend Rictor."

The gate opened a little ways down the beach and the three kids shot out of it at a full run. I smiled as a white blur followed and slipped in to trip the lead youngster. The other two tripped on the first and seven bundles of fur joined the pile. The Kilnyeri were two feet long and about a foot and a half tall.

"Some of the new people worry about your pets, friend Rictor."

"I don't think they need to worry," I said as the Kilnyeri darted in all directions. "Look at 'em."

The kids jumped back to their feet, and darted after the animals.

"It is true the creatures love the children," he returned. "I have been thinking about what you said about a new facility."

"And?"

"I have the ability to construct this facility but I have no way to create the Gestalts to staff it. It would take a Prime to do something like that. So far, my signals have gone unanswered. There are no Gestalts left that I can detect."

"I think you should begin construction, anyway, Jonny," I said. "There's a lot of world out there and we haven't covered even a tiny fraction of it. We may find others."

"Then I will send drones to explore the sea and find a likely spot, although I fear there will be no more Gestalts, friend Rictor. I fear that I am the last."

I glanced toward the tree line where Sadyuni was playing with...

The world slowed as I moved. The child was petting a Kilnyeri pup. My Kilnyeri were all much bigger. The underbrush shook violently as the mother charged into view. I could kill her but I was loathe to do it. I would before I let it hurt Yuni. Seven forms intercepted the mad Kilnyeri and blocked her path toward Yuni.

I landed right behind Yuni and pulled her up into my arms.

The mother hissed and the pup Yuni had been petting ran back to her. She stepped forward as if to attack and all seven hissed.

I'm not sure exactly how intelligent a Kilnyeri is, but they are smarter than any dog I have ever known. They certainly got their point across to the Kilnyeri mother.

We were their pack and not to be attacked.

The mother turned and herded four pups back into the trees.

"That was very interesting, friend Rictor."

"Yes it was," I said and let Yuni back down to run back toward the beach chasing Brynner through the sand. I had named them after the actors from a movie I had watched some years back, The Magnificent Seven.

The others followed except for two, Bronson and McQueen stayed near the trees to guard.

"I told you I didn't think they needed to worry about 'em."

"It seems you were correct, friend Rictor," he answered. "May I relay what has transpired here to the rest?"

"They need to know, I suppose," I said. "I hope they don't decide to nix these trips for the kids. I'm still getting used to the fact some animals don't run from us."

I settled into the leaves, just inside the trees to watch the kids play on the beach. Bronson and McQueen placed themselves to my right and left looking into the trees. Sometimes the Kilnyeri might be a nuisance but then they do something magnificent, and I realize they had been named quite aptly.

Chapter 40

"Do we take them?" Belinia asked.

"Yes," I answered.

In the canyon below our vantage point, a group of thirty Kresh'Far herded twelve Humans that looked to be teens.

"Not sure that we can return 'em to their homes, but we can at least get 'em to safety in Redoubt," I continued. "Wasn't planning to do any fighting on your first recruitment run, but let's do it."

Bel talked softly into her coms, "Sami, Bigosa, take your teams and come up on the left flank. Gharan and Ky take the right. We'll hit the front. The Prophet will shield the captives."

Very good. We had planned various strategies, while Bel was taking the advanced courses that Ruud taught. This was a good one for this situation. The teens were grouped tightly in the center. Easy for me to shield, while the others took out the Kresh.

If there had been a Wraith, I would have been tasked to burn him down, then shield the captives. He would not be left any time to act, and those bastards could move fast.

The teams moved into position.

"We go when the Prophet lands," she said.

I launched myself into the air, and landed right beside the teens, opening a shield around us.

The Kresh were startled, but turned toward me quickly, just in time to be hit from three different directions by Fourth Squad. It was a short fight as Fourth cut down the soldiers, before they even realized there was anyone besides me.

"Excellent job, Fourth," I said and turned to find the teens huddled in fear behind me. "I am not here to hurt you."

"Why did you kill the Masters?" a young girl wailed.

"They will never let us serve, after this," one of the boys said.

"You do not have to serve anyone," I said. "You are free to choose what you wish to do."

"We are bred to serve the Masters," a young man with red hair said. "We wish to serve."

"They will never let us serve them now," another said.

"Perhaps we can serve you," the red haired teen said. "We are strong and healthy."

He started to remove his clothing.

"Wait a minute, kid," I said. "What are you doing?"

"You must examine the property before you..."

"No I don't," I said. "Keep your clothes on."

Several of the others were in various stages of undressing.

"You will not take us?" a girl asked. I could see the despair in her eyes.

"You can come with us," I said. "But you are not slaves."

"We will serve you well, Master."

"Dear God," I muttered.

"We will get you settled in," Bel said. "Come."

"Yes, Master," the teens filed by me to join her.

"What is your name," she asked the red haired boy.

"I am Three," he said.

I looked back the way they had come. Somewhere out there was a group of people that looked as if they were raising their kids to be slaves for the Kresh. This sort of attitude was something taught to them by others. I needed more information before I could know for certain.

"Did you see what just happened, Jonny?"

"Yes, friend Rictor."

"I need to know where these people are, buddy," I said. "If what I fear is true, they need a little adjusting."

"There are fourteen villages along the line of travel these Kresh were following. Unless, of course, they turned at some point. Odds are quite high that they did."

"I still want to know where they are."

"Then we will find them, friend Rictor."

I nodded, "Bel, get these kids back to Redoubt. Keep them away from the others, until we can talk about their issues. Someone might try to take advantage of them."

"I expect some might, Prophet," she said. "They are...healthy and quite willing to share."

"I am going to backtrack this bunch as far as I can, and see if I can find where they came from. I have some serious issues with this situation."

"Your oath would not let you punish them, Prophet," she said. "Perhaps you should take a few of Fourth."

"I don't need to use my power to hurt them, Bel," I answered. "Spent a few years getting justice without violating that oath. I'll figure out what to do after I find them. Perhaps there is an explanation they can give me for this, that does not involve slave training their young to protect themselves from the Kresh 'harvest'."

She snarled, "Good luck with that, Prophet."

I let out a deep breath, "I hope they can explain. I've seen the rotten side of Humanity on my world. I'm surprised it took this long to find it here too."

"Up until recently, Sir, you have been seeing volunteers who wish to join us. There are many who didn't. We are seeing a few of those in Redoubt since the events at Varden. The longer you are out seeing the others this world has to offer, the more of this you will see. My father was from Therrasin before he was placed where you found us. There were many people there, and there was a great deal of corruption as well. I believe we will find many people who would rather serve the Kresh than join our cause."

"I expect so," I said. "What I want humanity to be and what it is are usually two very different things. I should not expect that to change, because I am on another world."

Chapter 41

"I cannot see any evidence of what you are looking for here," Jonny said. "My drone has been observing for two days, friend Rictor."

"I can't either, Jonny. This is the fourteenth one in their line of march. I'm afraid you were right, they must have turned at some point."

"I will keep looking with any spare drones, but there are hundreds of villages inside the triangle."

The Triangle was the area between the three Enclaves of Kresh that inhabited the area. They seemed to be the only ones who harvested the villages around us for slaves. Jonny was building a map of the area with his drones, but it took time.

"I don't see anything that suggests they're raising slaves here. But there's something off about the place," I said. "Look at the number of people. There are close to three hundred people either out in the fields, or inside the city."

"I count two hundred, and eighty-two, friend Rictor."

"Look at the buildings, Jonny. How do they house that many people with those few buildings? They'd have to be stacked like firewood inside there to house that many."

"You are correct, friend Rictor," he answered. "Do you wish to go inspect the village?"

"Not yet," I answered. "I need to get back, and deal with the issue of the kids we just brought in. They might be able to help us find the village they came from. This place is interesting, but I don't think they are the culprits."

"I will keep a drone in the area and watch this village, designated two hundred, and forty- five on our map."

"That's a good idea," I said. "Leave this one down here, and I will see you when I get home."

"Agreed," he said. "Travel safe, friend Rictor."

"Will do."

I liked the people in Redoubt, but I could use some time alone to think, and this trip gave me some of that time. There were going to have to be some things established with the folks in the facility. I had gone over a few of the defining points of freedom with them as we introduced them to Redoubt. But I needed to define exactly what I was trying to explain. Perhaps something like the Bill of Rights to define freedom to those who had never had it.

There would have to be a defined list of laws as well. The ones who joined the Guard had a set of rules to follow, Military Laws. The regular citizens were different. The good thing was that I had a good example to use as my guide. The United States Constitution and Bill of Rights would be a good starting point.

At the moment, we were a revolutionary organization. We would have to grow into something else to really succeed on Fhlo'Saa'Gellis. The Kresh had billions on the planet. Humans were probably just as numerous, they were just powerless.

My plan was to give them power, and a taste of the freedom they had been without for thousands of years.

Perhaps the Human race could take back that freedom. More than likely, we'd all get killed. The defining trait of my race was that we would try anyway. Ten thousand years, and the spirit hasn't been destroyed in them. They've been waiting for a chance to rise again, and I would do my best to give them that chance.

I started the long trek back to Redoubt. Even at the speed I could travel, it would take a while. I suppose I could run the distance at full speed, but it would risk being seen and I was on recon.

Chapter 42

"An abnormal amount of people entered this building," Jonny said as he outlined a building that rested near the bluff above village one forty-five.

"I should've thought of it sooner," I answered. "There must be a cave system inside that village. Which means they may still be our guilty party, at least where the kids are concerned. If the caves are big enough, they could conceal untold numbers inside."

"Unlikely, friend Rictor. I have spoken with the new arrivals since they have been kept from the general population of the facility. After the initial shock, they seem eager to please and willingly volunteered information whenever asked. They were raised outside, not in tunnels. They would be much paler of skin, if they had been kept in caves."

"True," I said. "I really want these people. Especially after what you relayed to me of the interviews by Belinia and Weriona. These kids were used for labor until they were old enough to be used for other things. I've seen the sex traffickers' trade on my world and it's a hell of a thing for youngsters to go through. From what they found out, it's only a single village involved with this."

"There have been questions from the others about the new arrivals," he said. "Friend Belinia has explained the situation, and why they will be held separate from the rest for a time. Why some of them are angry eludes me. I still have things to figure out about Humans."

"Who is angry?"

"Boligg has raised his voice against the decision," he said. "I think he is arguing because it was your decision to do it. My sensors did not detect the signs of true anger about it. Several others, Farthas and his followers, are truly angry, but have not revealed why that is so."

"Farthas is a weasel, Jonny. He and his ilk are who the kids need protection from. They would be the first to try to take what the youngsters would offer. Those kids need to know they aren't slaves anymore."

"If you wish, I would do this task, friend Rictor. I am one that has no physical temptation from their offers."

"That, my friend, is a wonderful idea."

"What is it you are writing, friend Rictor?"

"I'm trying to make a basic outline of what it means to be free. Back home we had the constitution of the United States and the Bill of Rights. I'm working from memory here and can't remember all the wording. It's been fifty years since I taught history."

"Bill of Rights?"

"It is a list of the Rights a person has in the United States that the government cannot take from its citizens," I said. "I need to get as much as I can remember down so we can start to formulate some sort of guide for those that join us."

"It will be quite some time before we need something like a government, friend Rictor."

"True, but it gives me something to pass the time with."

"I will gladly help with this list, friend Rictor."

"All right, the first one is freedom of speech. All are free to speak what they wish."

"That explains why you let Boligg and various others keep saying the things they do. I had wondered about this."

"They have a right to their views, Jonny, just as everyone else does."

"They can say anything?"

"Law and free speech have been at odds for the whole time the United States has been a country. Sometimes it is a pain in the ass, but can you be free without the right to say what you wish?"

"There must be laws as well friend Rictor."

"Definitely. They are free to say what they will, but they have to stay within the law."

"This is going to be a very complex system," he said.

"Indeed, and that's just the first. Then there is the right to bear arms. This is one of the issues the United States government has been arguing about for decades. Some parties wish to restrict guns, and others do not. But it plainly states that the Bill of Rights is a list of rights that cannot be infringed upon by the government."

"Everyone has weapons, already, Friend Rictor."

"And this is a right of each one of them that will not be taken away. Unless, of course, they use this right to break the law. The system is complex, as you said, but I've seen it create a great country on Earth."

"You have spoken of the United States of America many times," he said. "Is there not strife amongst them?"

"There will always be strife between those who want to rule themselves, and those who wish to rule everyone."

"Then when we present this to the others, we should try to present a clear, and structured document. Your knowledge, of where this has gone over centuries, should be invaluable to the creation of your Bill of Rights."

"Our Bill of Rights, Jonny."

"As you say."

Chapter 43

"This is all we know, Master."

"Never call me Master, Three," I said. "You have no Master."

He nodded but I could see no true belief. The kid had been through the grinder. I had heard his interviews with Bel and Weriona, so I didn't need to ask details about what was done to him.

"I know what the adults did to you, Three. I know you expect the same here. I need you to understand that you have a choice, boy. Did you enjoy what they did to you?"

"Sometimes," he said slowly.

"So if I told you that you can say no, what would you do?"

"I am afraid to answer," his face was pale.

"You don't have to fear me, boy."

"I would say no."

"That is exactly where you stand here in Redoubt. When you say no, it means they cannot make you do things anymore."

"I can offer you something more, though. You've seen what my Guards can do."

"You would let us? We have been forbidden to touch weapons of any kind."

"When your training with Jonny is finished, those who wish to join my Guards will have that opportunity. He will let each of you know what it involves, and what would be expected of you. You will be able to choose what you wish to do after training. Join the Guard, or work in hydroponics, or livestock. You can even choose to continue education with Jonny and Relki. You can also choose to leave here, and go to another village."

His head shake was understandable at the last choice, but he needed to know the choices available.

"As for now, can you help me? I need to know more about this crèche you were raised in. I know you don't know how to get to it, but if you can give me some details about it, perhaps Jonny can find it."

His eyes widened, "You are not taking us back there, are you?"

"Absolutely not," I said. "But there are over two hundred kids there being raised to give to the Kresh, and I won't abide that."

He jerked back as a little of the anger I held in check slipped at the thought of these people. My eyes may have flamed just a little.

"What do you intend to do?" he asked.

I was truly happy he was thinking, instead of blurting out whatever I asked. His classes with Jonny were showing.

"Honestly, I'm not sure," I answered. "I intend to remove those kids from the village, certainly. What to do with the villagers, I'm not so sure about just yet."

"I have children in the crèche," he said. "I will see my sons again?"

"Most definitely, Three."

He nodded, "What do you need to know that might help, Mas... Prophet?"

"Describe everything you know about the village. Where the buildings are placed, how they are shaped, what each building is used for, and any landmarks. How many fields surround the village? What crops were being grown? I understand you, and the others were used in the fields, until you reached the age where you could be used for other things. What did you wear when you worked in the fields? Was it different from what the rest of the village wore? Any detail will help us."

"These are questions I can answer!" his excitement was a dramatic change from the fear he was feeling before.

"Why did we not think of this in the early interviews?" Jonny said in my ear.

I typed into the tablet he had given me upon entering the room to interview Three.

It read, "You've been at this for a year, Jonny. I've been at it for eighty."

"The crèche is in a large building shaped like this," he held his fingers in the shape of an L. "The girl's crèche is also shaped like this, but it is across the village from ours."

"Great," I said. "Keep going."

"There are ten fields with several crops. Each year we would alternate the crops so the soil would not be stripped. Each crop would feed the soil in a different way. North of the village are three fields. One has...."

Chapter 44

I sat on the outcropping watching the screaming kids once more running along the beach.

"Quite a few more kids out here than last time, Prophet."

"There are almost enough to have to split this up in two separate shifts," I said.

Rolan sat on the outcropping a few feet lower than I, "It does us all good to get out here with something besides hunting Kresh in mind."

"I believe it. Too bad Fourth drew the short straw and had to do guard duty."

He laughed, "Yeah, that's too bad."

"Laugh while you can," I said. "Next guard shift is First Squad's turn."

"Look out, Munseizer!" Rolan yelled as a forty pound ball of furry death plowed into his back and darted past the fallen Guard.

He was instantly back on his feet and pursuing the Kilnyeri. It darted to the left just as Munseizer pulled something from the harness on his back.

"Oh shit, is that a lasso?" I muttered.

The Kilnyeri shot to the right, and the rope whirled above the running Guard's head. In an instant, it shot forward, and the rope hit just in front of the Kilnyeri, who stepped right into the loop.

Munseizer yelled in triumph as the loop tightened on the Kilnyeri's front legs and it rolled forward across the beach. He was on the animal in a split second, and before Bronson even knew what was happening, he was tied, upside down in the sand with all four legs strapped together.

Bronson rolled in the sand for a few moments and gave up his struggle. Munseizer patted the Kilnyeri on his head and untied the rope.

"I'll be damned," I said as Bronson shot off into the woods, "Who knew Munseizer was a cowboy? I guess that explains the bowed legs."

"Yes, Prophet," Rolan said. "He was what you would call a cowboy on Shintarra. They are herders, raising large amounts of livestock."

"I think Bronson is going to make another try at him," I said as the trees shook before the Kilnyeri was shooting across the sand like a bullet.

"Looks like he brought company," Rolan returned as the trees shook again and four more forms joined Bronson.

What happened next was some of the most impressive feats of dexterity I have ever seen this side of Colin's Dance of Blades.

Munseizer was gone when the Kilnyeri hit where he had been, but his rope snatched Bronson from the air. This wasn't too surprising, but when he looped the other four in the coils of that rope, and pounced on the squirming pile of Kilnyeri, my mouth dropped.

Rolan exploded in laughter, and several others who had seen it stood gaping. Not many of them get to have one over on one of the Kilnyeri. To see four bested with a rope was wonderful.

When the furry pile ceased its squirming, Munseizer released them. They ran in four directions.

They weren't done. The other three had seen what was going on, and all seven began running in circles around the cowboy, his rope swinging around him in circles.

The rope would lash out, and the Kilnyeri would try to dodge.

"That was close," Rolan said.

"They're learning to watch the rope," I said.
"Smarter than they have any right to be."
"No doubt."
"Now how did he know which way that little turd was going to jump?" he asked.
"I have no idea, but he's catching them more than he's missing," I said. "The man has no idea what he started. They'll never leave him alone now."
"He is enjoying the game as much as they are, Prophet."
"True enough," I returned. "Wonder who will give out first."
"Care to lay a wager on the results?"
"You've been hanging out with the Yevinn'Tor bunch too much."
"They do like their wagers," he laughed.
We had six Guards from Yevinn'Tor. They were all large people, over six feet tall. They all seemed to wager on almost anything.
"Speaking of the Yevinns, I've noticed you spending a lot of time with a certain Team leader."
"I don't seem to be having a great deal of luck with her, Sir," he said. "I think she has a problem with my size. She's just too nice to say she does not like dwarves."

He had a point. Rolan was maybe an inch under five feet and Tar'Weelus was six and a half feet tall.

"If things change, make sure to report it, Rolan. We'll transfer one of you to another squad. I have no problem with relationships, but they need to be under separate commands."

"Understood, Sir," he said. "But it looks like you won't have to worry about it. Not that I won't keep trying."

I chuckled.

"Persistence might make up for height," he said.

Chapter 45

"How is it I have not even reached a state of blur?" Tar'Weelus complained.

"Perhaps you are not drinking enough," Lumet'Yre answered as the dice rolled across the floor. "Ahaa! I can remedy that situation, Tar. Drink!"

The large blonde woman raised an enormous cup of clear liquid to drain it dry.

I knew the clear liquid was this world's equivalent to vodka. It was made from the not-potato.

She lowered the glass and patiently waited for the effects to come, "It does no good! The burn even disappears in seconds!"

She snatched up the dice that looked to have eight sides and rolled. She glared at the roll of three eights and two sixes. Atir'Ylas, another of the Yevinns, retrieved the dice and rolled. His roll was three threes, a one, and a four.

"That was pitiful Atir," Ky'Tellin laughed and retrieved the dice.

"Piss off, Ky," was his answer.

"The Prophet's language has so many handy phrases," Zulijah'Fein laughed.

"You can piss off, too, Zuli," he said as she took the dice after Ky'Tellin rolled.

"Poor thing," she said and rolled.

Atir'Ylas cursed.

"Many handy phrases," she said. "I think that was referring to the sexual organ of a pack animal?"

"That it was," I said and walked out of the shadows.

"Greetings, Prophet," Zulijah'Fein said. "Drink, Atir. We are not to be distracted by pesky Prophets and such. We are about the serious business of getting, what was that word?"

"Shit-faced," Atir'Ylas answered.

"I hate to be the one to inform you all this, but when you tied your streams you made your bodies heal faster than the alcohol can affect you."

"What are you saying, Prophet of...Evil?" Zulijah'Fein asked in alarm. "You are saying we cannot reach the blur?"

"Afraid so."

Atir'Ylas cursed. For a long time.

"This should have been in the introduction, Prophet," Lumet'Yre said with a sad look on his face.

"Perhaps not," Tar'Weelus returned. "You would have no volunteers. How do you think we survive this awful world? Alcohol... Prophet.... Alcohol."

"I suppose it is now our duty to keep this horrible secret," Ky'Tellin said in misery. "If it were common knowledge, the volunteers would cease to join. Then our army would never truly become an army, and we would have made this sacrifice in vain. Much better for them to join us in our misery."

"It's a hard thing to ask of you," I said. "But the whole Freedom Movement depends on you brave souls to keep this from the others."

"Excuse me, friend Rictor," Jonny said. "I am ninety-eight percent certain I have found the village we have been searching for."

My head snapped up, "Numbers?"

"Yes, friend Rictor."

"Excellent news. I'll be up to the control room in a minute."

"He has found the village?" Tar'Weelus asked.

"Yes."

"I request to be part of the patrol that goes with you, Prophet. What we have learned of the Numbers goes against everything a Yevinn believes. We would truly love to be part of the justice brought to that place."

Ky'Tellin was nodding, "Children, Prophet. Children are sacred. Not to be used as..."

"I understand," I said. "And I agree wholeheartedly. Let me get the information, and I will get back to you on the details. Please go inform First and Fourth to begin preparation."

Chapter 46

"I understand you plan to go attack a village," Boligg sneered. "All your talk of freedom, and you are going to force your beliefs on another innocent village..."

"Boligg!" Huynini growled. "One more word! I'll throw you out the damn airlock myself."

"I'll never understand this blind trust you put in him," he pointed at me.

My left eye was twitching.

"Come with me," she ordered and literally dragged him down the hall. "I'll catch up with you, Prophet. I need to show this ignorant bastard something."

"We'll wait," I said.

She nodded and continued down the hall.

"She's taking him to the Numbers?" Yemelle of First Squad asked.

"The airlock is in that direction," Bollinger returned.

"Shall we wager?" Tar'Weelus asked.

"Damn Yevinns will bet on anything," Belinia said. "I would wager the Numbers, personally. Huynini is too nice to just throw him out of an airlock."

"Obviously you haven't worked much with her," Bollinger said. "She's as sweet as they come, but she has a very low tolerance for stupid. I'm about fifty-fifty on this one."

"He has a daughter," Atir'Ylas returned. "That will certainly figure into this wager."

"She has passed the airlock, friend Rictor," Jonny said. I sighed in relief.

"Numbers, it is," I said. "I was a little worried about that airlock. The temptation had to be strong."

"I would have used the airlock," Rolan shrugged.

"I would worry more about the return trip," Munseizer said. "If what he sees doesn't alter his line of thinking, she'll probably throw him out. It depends on how stupid the man truly is."

"The problem isn't stupidity," I said. "The man hates me, and will go the opposite direction I go just for spite. If she breaks through that, I'll be impressed."

"If talking to one of those kids doesn't change his argument, nothing will," Jilna said. "I can't believe people can be that awful."

"I've seen plenty of it over the years," I said. "You would be surprised."

"People will do horrible things, Jilna," Yarnust said. "Whole keeps have been destroyed, the men crucified, women raped and killed, and the children enslaved on Parlais by other Lords."

"They are ordered by the Masters who they are to destroy," Freijan Mols, another Parlaisian said. "But some of them do enjoy the work the Masters order."

"She has taken him to talk to friend Thirty-two."

I could imagine what Boligg was about to hear, Huynini was a smart woman. Thirty-two was a tiny blonde girl who just turned eighteen years old. Boligg had a daughter of twelve years.

Thirty-two had her first child at age twelve. She didn't know who the father was because she had been used by forty-three different men throughout the time she had conceived. They had done this to a twelve year old, and it made my blood boil. Even worse, she was raised expecting this to happen. She didn't even understand it was wrong. It was just life. The boys were used just as badly as the girls. It would truly take all of my will to keep from destroying that place and leaving an ash pile.

"Let's return to the Rec Center and give her a few minutes," I said. "This could take a while."

"Should we leave a guard on the airlock?" Belinia asked.

"I have complete trust in the First Guard. If she decides to use the airlock, the man is truly a lost cause."

Chapter 47

Nearly fifty heads turned as Boligg crossed the Rec Center on his way to the living quarters. His face was pale, and his eyes were puffy. He refused to even look in the direction of the squads as we waited for Huynini to return.

"Damn," Bollinger said, "extra guard duty next week."

"You actually wagered she would throw him out?" Kord, Tar'Weelus' second team member asked.

"I would have done it weeks ago along with Farthas and his bunch," he returned. "Did you know Jonny caught them trying to sneak into the quarters where the girls were housed right after we brought them in?"

"I rectified that particular issue, friend Bollinger," Jonny said. "I showed the men the new addition I have built in the bottom most floor of the facility. The Prophet and I were discussing Rights and Laws, and the delicate balance between the two. I asked what they did to people who broke those laws, and he told me of the prison system. I began to construct one."

"Really?" Bollinger asked.

"I took Farthas down and showed him the small room that would be his home from this point forward, if he chose to continue down the path he was walking. Then I showed him the videos of all the various things he has stolen from his fellow inhabitants. I think he has a better understanding of what he can and cannot do now."

I grinned, "You tell 'em, Sheriff."

I had been completely unaware of Jonny's actions, but I happened to agree with his choices on the subject.

"What are you lazy dorgs waiting on?" Huynini stood in the door.

"I think the word is dugs," Belinia answered. "Or ducks. No, ducks are birds that swim... Dogs!!! That's it."

"Whatever," Huynini shrugged, "Let's go you lazy dogs. And what are you grinning about, Prophet? You should have been halfway to the target. I'm guessing you waited to see if I would use the airlock or not. Who wagered? I know some of the Yevinns had to have placed bets."

"I know nothing of any wagers," Tar'Weelus said.

I snorted as the squads filed out of the large room past Huynini.

As I walked past her she said, "He is a much better person than the one you see, Prophet. He has a history that made him what he is."

"I'll take your word for it, First Guard," I said. "He's never shown me anything but hate."

"I know, and it is infuriating," she said. "He's from Terajewid, a small population world. They live in family compounds and do various trades, mining, farming, or herding. His family tried to stand up for themselves, and the Masters destroyed it all. They killed, and ate every member of his family right in front of him. Then they leveled the compound, and killed every animal."

"Jesus," I muttered.

"They took this teenager, after doing that, and dragged him away to another world. There they threw him into a village as an example of what happens."

"And he wonders why we want to fight them?"

"Oh he wants to kill them all, my Prophet," she said. "He is convinced he, and his family are now doomed by the actions of someone standing up to them again. He is jealous of the power we have to fight back, and hates himself, and us for that jealousy. There is much going on inside that man."

"I look at the people on this world, Huynini, and I see this story repeated. Over and over, I see it, and it drives me crazy. I know what people can be if they try. I just want to give them the option to try, if they want to. They must have the choice of whether they'll fight or not. Choosing to defend the scum we're about to go after is a choice as well. If he hates me so much that he'll do that, I will repatriate him in another village, where he can be whoever he chooses to be. If he truly believes they should be allowed to do what they're doing, he will most certainly be removed from here."

"He does not believe that, my Prophet," she said. "He tried to leave within a minute of hearing Thirty-two began telling of her childhood. I held him in that seat for the whole thing, and told him there were eleven more life stories to hear. He begged me to let him go, and the last words he spoke to me were asking forgiveness."

"I'll let you be the judge on this, Huynini," I said. "I've listened to his shit as much as I intend to."

"I have the impression he will not be giving you so much trouble, my Prophet."

Chapter 48

"Are you sure this is the one?" Gers asked.

We looked from the top of a tree across a clearing from the outbuildings of the village.

"Everything looks normal enough," Stelgar added.

"They don't look like monsters, do they?" I answered. "Watch them for a bit, and I think their true colors will come out....or we can follow First Guard."

Huynini strode out of the trees.

"Looks like she has a plan," Gers said.

Belinia was only a step behind her. I dropped out of the tree, where I had been perched, and joined my two team leaders.

"You know I spent a great deal of time convincing myself not to do exactly what you two are doing."

"Why in the seventh level of Rashid's Hell would you do that?"

"You been learning new curses from Krole?" I asked.

"Maybe," Huynini answered. "They are so eloquent."

"I like that one," Bel returned.

"This is what I wanted to do from the beginning," I said. "First Squad, take the Number crèche on the left. Fourth will take the crèche on the right. I have little doubt this is the place. When you confirm the presence of the Numbers, set up guard around the crèche, and remove anyone who can be a danger to the kids from the premises. No killing. I have something in mind for these bastards."

Huynini moved to take her position to my left, and Bel took the right. We crossed the clearing in two columns. I heard the villagers ahead as they rushed to be in a position to meet us.

"Go," I said and the squads split to each side, and shot into the village at a run.

I kept on walking forward on the original track, right down the center of the main street through town toward a gathering mob of people.

A large bearded man with a sword strapped to his back strode forward to meet me.

"You are not welcome here!" he yelled. "We have sent a messenger to the Masters!"

"Jonny?"

"No one has left the village, friend Rictor."

I moved so fast the man didn't even see me until I was less than a foot away, and he walked into me. He impacted my chest, and fell backwards. I was unmoved.

"I have come because there have been stories of a village that raises children to be slaves," I said. "I heard this, and thought 'What a despicable thing to do.' I could probably get past that, considering the threat of the Masters over a village. Then I hear that this village, not content with just raising these children to be given to the Kresh, has been abusing those very children."

I stepped forward again as the big man stood, and he stumbled backward once more.

"All of this has been confirmed by the latest of that village's gifts to the Kresh. If I were to find out what village would do such things to children, I'm not certain if I could allow that village to survive."

"The Masters..." the big man started.

A volley of ten fiery disks slammed into the ground around the man, "Silence!"

"Confirmation," Bel informed in my ear.

"Second confirmation," Huynini said. "Girl's crèche secured."

"Boy's crèche secured."

"It seems my teams have found two build-ings full of children, right here, in this village."

The bearded man drew the huge sword from his back, and I stood motionless as he swung it. It was an impressive swing, aimed to cleave down through me from the left shoul-der where it joined my neck, and down into my chest. A foot away from my shoulder, I caught the blade in my gloved hand. Ripping it from his grasp, I snapped the blade in two with my single hand.

"Now you will gather everyone in this vil-lage, right here, right now, in this square. No need to worry about the kids who have num-bers for names. We'll gather those."

Chapter 49

"Never wanted to break my oath any more than I do right now," I muttered as the children filed past. The older kids carried the younger.

There was a group of the Numbers who needed help walking away from the crèche. No less than fifteen girls who looked to range from twelve or so to eighteen were pregnant. Some of these were very pregnant.

Another group of the kids needed help for another reason. My eyes were beginning to burn with the flames of my anger, as these children limped, or were carried from the crèche with bruises covering their bodies.

Last to come from the crèche were twenty people of various ages, who had been caged in the rear of each crèche. Twelve men, bruised and battered, and eight women in much the same shape.

"You will never get away with...erk!"

I had covered the ten feet between myself, and the Overman. He dangled above the ground, my hand gripping his throat.

"The very thought that you still draw breath offends me," I growled. "Push me one bit more, and I will remove that offense."

I threw the big man back into the crowd of villagers, bowling over three of his followers. I had wondered how something like this could even exist. There had to be some good people dropped off in the place.

Then I saw that last group of people, and I understood.

"If you would accompany the Numbers out of the village, Prophet, I would gladly remove the offense you currently speak of."

Huynini was standing by my side. She continued, "Your oath may demand you leave these..."

She looked at the villagers with disgust, "...animals alive. I have no such restrictions."

"I have a plan."

"It better be a good one, my Prophet," she said as the last of the injured prisoners were helped along the street past us.

"First, Fourth, escort these folks to their new home. When you arrive, send word, and I will drop the shield."

"What shield?" Bel asked.

"This one," I answered, opening the portal in my stream for the shield I had built around the center square, surrounding the villagers.

"As you can see," I said to the villagers, "My people would rather have your blood than to see you survive this day. Lucky for you, I have a different plan. From this day forth, you are your own pool of slaves for the Masters. You will remain in this village. If you try to leave, we will find you, and return you to this place. You try to enslave another person as you have done these children, and we will return. You have been judged by your peers, and have been found wanting. This is your fate, your sentence."

I walked to the column of people filing into the trees, "Where you are going, this sort of thing will not be tolerated. You will be safe there. If there is anything you need from the village before you go, let any of my Guards know. We will collect anything you may need."

"First, gather blankets and any clothing you can find to take for them. It may be a little chilly at night. You find any food that's easily portable, take it. Keep your scouts out, this is a large group."

"I have three drones closing on your position," Jonny said in my ear.

"Excellent," I said. "Keep an eye out for 'em, Jonny."

"I will, friend Rictor."

It took twelve days to get the numbers back to redoubt. I spent the whole twelve days watching things fall apart inside the shield. It was quite a show. Reminded me of watching a movie on a big screen back home, except this wasn't fake. It was reality for this group of, what had Yemelle called them? Grostachs. Beasts. Occasionally I would throw an olnyaq from the town's pens inside for them to eat. There was a well in the center of the square so they didn't lack for water.

The first day, they were sullen, the next they threatened what the Masters would do to me, and all of my people when they told them what I had done. The fifth day they began to scream, and fight amongst themselves. I shook my head as they fell on one another.

I expected them to self-destruct over a matter of months or years. When I walked from that place on the twelfth day, a third of them remained. Ninety people were thirty, and I had an unrelenting craving for popcorn.

Chapter 50

"The sheer number of them means we cannot keep them all separate from the others," Huynini said.

"Many of the younger children are not emotionally scarred yet," Weriona returned. "They should be able to be placed with some of the others in Redoubt."

"Up until now they have been cared for by the older Numbers," Three said. "If you take them away, it will be harder on the older kids than if you let them continue to care for the younger children."

I had been listening to them and hadn't even noticed when Three had been standing behind me.

"He has a point," I said, turning to Three. "Perhaps you should be the one to set up our new arrangements, Three."

He stepped back a step, shook his head and stepped back forward. I could see the conflict in the boy. He'd come far since the first Numbers had beeen brought to Redoubt.

"It would be much easier on them, if they saw a familiar face doing things for them. It will take time to get past the feeling of help-lessness they are having right now."

"What would you suggest?" Huynini asked.

"I have an idea if you are amenable", Three said.

"Tell me," I said.

Five hours later, Three entered a large chamber we had prepared for the Numbers. The children filed into the room to see a series of long tables laden with food. There were various roasted meats, platters of vegetables, and piles of fruits. Three lined the Numbers around the room.

"We welcome you to Redoubt," I said.

Their attention turned to me, even as their mouths watered at the sight of the food. I think they expected to serve whoever would be eating this feast.

"I understand you have been rather limited, as to what you have experienced," I waved my arms toward the tables. "This is for you. Sit where you will. Eat what you want. Rest and recuperate from the trip."

I sat at one of the tables, and reached out for a piece of the roasted olnyaq. Placing it on my plate, I spooned some of the not-potato in a sweet gravy onto the plate.

They watched me, but remained in place.

"This is truly for us?"

I looked up to see a boy of about ten years, across the table from me.

"Absolutely," I answered, motioning to the bench across from me. "Sit, eat."

He sat, and slowly reached for a piece of the olnyaq. I think he expected to be hit. When the olnyaq was on his plate, he looked terrified.

"You should try some of these," I said, rising. He cringed, but the expected strike never came. "They are delicious."

I spooned some of the not-potatoes onto his plate.

He took a small bite, still expecting the strike he just knew was coming.

I don't think they had even eaten meat before, and I could see the amazement on his face at the new taste. Glancing to my left, I saw another child walk slowly toward the table.

It took almost an hour to get them all situated. I spent that hour serving food to them. They were all amazed at the new flavors, and some of them didn't even cringe at my approach.

It was educational for me to see it first hand, and it made any thoughts of pity for the village that caused this to slip away.

"You do not need to serve me, Prophet," Three said as he sat beside the boy who remained across from my seat.

"You, most of all, Three," I returned. "You are the architect of all this. It was a wonderful idea. What would you like?"

I returned to my seat after setting Three up with his plate.

"I have spent the last hours telling my people what you have done, here, Prophet," he said.

"Did you find your children?"

"Yes, they are healthy. Do you see Eighty-Nine? She is the one with the long black hair. She is on the very end of my row."

"Yes."

"The three young ones on this side of her are my children."

"Is she their mother?"

"Yes, she is the mother of all three."

"That wasn't the normal outcome was it?"

"No, Prophet," he said. "Usually we were paired at random. I made deals with others to change places whenever I could. She is special."

I smiled, "That is something I understand, my friend. I understand it well."

Chapter 51

"He's using the axe wrong," Gers stated. "He should grip it closer to the end."

"Really?" I answered. "That's the first thing you notice?"

"No, Sir," He answered with a grin. "There are twelve men in the logging crew. Most of them are using their tools as they were designed, except the third from the right. He is gripping the axe to close to the head."

Gers had poked his head up for about three seconds, just as I had done. It was a sort of focus training he couldn't get at Redoubt.

"How many pack animals?"

"Four."

I grinned

"Good job, Gers."

"Thank you, Prophet."

"How did you know he was holding the axe wrong? I had no clue."

"On Bollivar, before the Masters came for me, I was a Woodcutter. I have had an axe in my hand from the age of ten, Sir."

"That explains that behemoth of an axe you keep in your quarters, I suppose."

"Ruud has us training every third day with our unique weapon."

"I saw some of that a few months ago. Saw you using that axe, and Krole with his scythe. Why don't you carry it with you?"

"We thought you would be offended if we did not use your Soulguard weapon."

"Shit, Gers, use what is comfortable. There are places where the swords would be better replaced with the axe. We focus on the swords because they are well suited to us as we fight in groups. You ever need that axe, you should have it handy."

"Yes, Sir," he said. "Did you have a weapon you would preferred to use before becoming a Soulguard?"

"Carried an M-14 for a good bit," I answered, "but that's not something I can do here. Nowadays, I am my extra weapon."

"I can see that," he grinned. "I certainly wish you could train us to do that."

"Rash'Tor'Ri can do that. I can't."

"I truly wish to meet this Rash'Tor'Ri someday, Prophet."

"Perhaps, someday, we can all sit and have a beer together," I said.

"That would be an interesting meeting, Prophet."

"True enough," I said, turning to Huynini. "Alright, First. Regular recruitment run to begin with. I'll remain in the back."

"Yes, my Prophet," she said and started down the embankment toward the woodcutters.

Gers and Stelgar, her fire team, followed closely. The rest of First Squad joined them with me in the rear.

"Greetings," the first of the woodcutters said as we approached. His eyes moved to the twin sword hilts protruding above their shoulders, "I am guessing you are the ones we've been warned about?"

"I imagine so," Huynini said. "We are the Prophet's Guards. We are here to see if any of your people are interested in learning how to stand up to the Masters. If you would be so kind, would you go in, and ask if your village is amenable to speaking with us? We will not intrude where we are unwelcome."

"I can tell you we were warned that any contact with you would spell our doom," he grinned. "We were doomed the day they took us from our worlds. Not such a large threat, after all. I will go inform the others that you are here. I will return shortly."

He nodded and strode toward the village.

"How many trees do you plan to take down, here?" she asked another of the woodcutters.

He pointed to the line of trees they were working on, "We plan to take these down and work in through the warm season so we need not cut in winter. The larger trees will be used for burning. The medium sized logs are used for building."

"Gers," Huynini said. "What say we cut a few for these folks?"

Gers grinned and picked up the axe that the woodcutter who had gone into the village had leaned on the tree. He hefted it in his hands to get the feel for it, and pushed his Soul out into the tool.

For a Guard, he swung the axe gently, taking a large chunk from one side. Then a stronger swing from the other and a tree fell. The woodcutters looked on with awe.

"May I?" Huynini asked one of them, motioning toward his axe.

He handed it to her with eyebrows raised in surprise.

"The v cut is where the tree falls?" she asked Gers.

"Yes, Ma'am."

She swung after imbuing the axe. It bit deep and she swung again to leave a notch cut in the trunk. Moving to the other side she swung and splinters exploded from the opposite side. The tree fell.

"A little hard, Ma'am," Gers said. "You'd make a fine Lumberjack with a little training."

She moved to the next one and felled it perfectly.

"Very little training," he laughed.

"They call her the First Guard for a reason," added Stelgar, as he stepped over to ask for one of their axes.

Others joined them. By the time the first woodcutter returned First Squad had taken down thirty trees of various sizes for the woodcutters. Gers gave pointers to the others as they learned to fall a tree in the proper manner.

"The others would meet with you," the first woodcutter said. "My name is Thusarin, formerly of Cerres. Currently a chrinor member of the village of Jarnou."

Huynini nodded, "Lukell, Atir'Ylas, take your teams, and set up a perimeter. We don't need a repeat of Varden."

Varden was the name of the village who had needed to evacuate because of our presence. Some of them had been nothing but trouble from the beginning.

"Yes Ma'am."

Both teams slipped off into the forest.

"She has become quite good at her job," Jonny said in my ear from coms.

"That she has, Jonny."

Chapter 52

We followed the group of woodcutters down the slope into the village. Interestingly, they took us straight to the building where we guessed there would be caverns. I had wondered if they would try to hold this as a secret.

"This is one of the reasons we are already doomed, if the Masters look too closely at us," said Thusarin. "If they enter this building, we are done."

I stepped through the door to see the whole back side of the building extend into the rocks of the bluff it was built against.

"I thought as much," I muttered.

"That is a fairly large cavern," Jonny said in my ear. "It could easily hold the numbers we have seen through the drones."

"I am sorry for the ruse," Thusarin said. "I am a little more than a minor member of Jarnou. I am a woodcutter by choice and the Overman of Jarnou by the choice of the others. I mean no offense, Lady, but I would like to speak to the Prophet, himself."

He turned to me, "Your reputation has preceded you, Prophet. The burn scars are pretty easy to recognize."

"Sometimes that doesn't seem to be a good thing, Thusarin," I said, stepping forward to grasp his hand. "I am Rictor Hughes. They call me the Prophet."

I motioned toward First Squad.

"When you say 'choice of the others', you mean they voted for you?"

"That is exactly what he means," another voice came from the shadows. Two people came forward. One an old man, the other a young woman who helped the man.

The most surprising part was the man spoke in English, "I am Sergeant George J Avery of the United States Army. Some of what I've heard about the speeches you've been givin' reminds me of some of my country's history."

"It should, Sergeant," I laughed. "I took a lot of it straight from the history books. Before joining the Soulguard, I was Master Sergeant Rictor H Hughes of the United States Marine Corp."

"Soulguard, eh?" he asked. "Met some of you boys in Laos."

"I met my first Soulguard in 'Nam," I said, "where they recruited me."

"Interestin' bunch," he said. "Talkin' about focus and faith made me a little nervous, and I declined the offer. By the looks of you, I may have made a mistake. Too old for all that now."

"It's still the same thing today, Sergeant," I said. "Focus and faith does the trick. As long as your mind still works, it's never too late. Of course, the fight we are starting will probably kill us all."

"Boy, you give me my strength again, and I'll be right beside you."

"Father," the girl helping him chastised the old man.

"Girl, don't you go givin' me a hard time," he groused. "We have a lot of things here that can help you, Master Sergeant. Thusarin can show it to you. I'm too old to be getting around down there."

"Down there?"

"We discovered some things under the ground as we dug this chamber. We try to only have a certain amount of people outside at any given moment. There are things your people may have never seen. It's old technology."

"You may be surprised what we've seen," I said with a grin.

Chapter 53

We followed along behind Thusarin as he proceeded deeper into the cavern. At the rear of the cavern there was a shack. I had to admit, my curiosity was peaked. He opened the door and I felt a familiar cool breeze. It felt like the circulation system in Redoubt.

"Jonny, are you seeing this?" I asked.

Thusarin looked at me oddly when none of the others answered.

"Gers, step out and tell Jonny we need a couple of sensors so he can see this as we do."

"Yes, Sir."

"We need to wait a second, Thusarin, if you don't mind."

"Alright," he nodded. He was obviously curious.

Gers entered the building with two small sensor platforms. One he placed just inside the building, the other he brought toward us.

"Just inside the door should be sufficient, friend Gers," Jonny said.

Thusarin's eyes widened at the voice coming from the sensor platform. A slow grin spread across his face.

"Perhaps you may not be as surprised at what we have discovered after all, Prophet."

"Lead on, Thusarin," I said.

He nodded, and we continued into the opening behind the makeshift shack. About thirty feet in, the corridor opened into another tunnel.

"This was cut by machines, Prophet," Stelgar said. "No hand tools did this."

Stelgar would know since he'd spent his early years on Strahena working in the mines.

Thusarin nodded, "We had much the same thought upon finding this tunnel. Or so they tell me. It was located just before I was deposited in the village above by the Masters."

"How long ago was that?" I asked.

"Eleven years," he answered. "George took a liking to me almost immediately, and I started working with him. He was the Overman at the time. Five years ago, he decided he needed to step down due to his age. I was elected by the village to continue his work."

While explaining this, Thusarin proceeded down the sloping tunnel, deeper into the mountain. The torches reflected from shiny metal ahead. He approached a door much like the doors in Redoubt. You wouldn't know it was there if you weren't used to the small difference between the wall and door.

"When they found it, it was open."

He rapped on the outer surface in a pattern I recognized quite well.

"Shave and a haircut...two bits," I muttered.

"You truly are from Doran," he said. "We don't see many people from your world here."

"They've been having a difficult time taking as many from there," I said. "We've been interfering for over a thousand years."

The door slid open slowly. It stopped close to the edge of the wall. The doors in Redoubt completely retracted. As we followed him through the door I could see why. There was a handle attached to the inside of the door.

"How did you get that to stay?" Stelgar asked.

"We have found some interesting things down inside the facility," Thusarin said. "This was an adhesive we located. All of the doors have the handles attached with it."

"I have used this many times," Jonny said in my ear.

Inside were two men that practically bristled with weapons.

"Overman," the first one greeted our guide.

"Sagan," he returned.

"Is it him?"

"Yes it is."

A smile crossed the big man's face, "We've been waiting a while for you, Prophet."

I nodded to him, "This is so much more than I was expecting when I woke up this morning."

Thusarin handed Sagan the torch he had been carrying. Sagan doused it and touched a panel beside the door. Lights powered up but were dim. Still brighter than the torch, though.

"You've got power," Huynini said with a smile.

"Some of us are familiar with the workings in Hub. We know there are ways to start the power generators, but lack the knowledge to do so. Our power comes from a generator that is not actually running. It is a mystery."

"See if he will take you to the generator, friend Rictor," Jonny said.

"Patience, Jonny," I answered.

"Understood, friend Rictor."

"What does your mysterious friend wish to see, Prophet?"

"He wants to see the generator, amongst a million other things," I said with a grin. "We have time for that after you finish your tour."

"I will be glad to add that, and anything else you would like to see to the tour."

"If this place is anything like Redoubt, there should be a room filled with databanks. Possibly many rooms. He would really love to see if any of his kind still survive," I said. "We are doubtful because of the power shortage, but it's something of great importance to my friend. Therefore of great importance to me, as well."

"Then we will show you this room. Describe what the room looks like in this Redoubt you speak of."

Chapter 54

"I'm sorry, Jonny," I said, looking at the dead databank. "I know this wasn't what you wanted to see."

"It was much to hope for, friend Rictor," he answered. "I did not expect the Gestalt to be alive with the low amount of power that seems to be available to the facility. It appears to only have housed one Gestalt. Will you ask if you can bring the memory bank to me so I can learn what it knew?"

"I'm sure he will let me if it doesn't hurt the power output for the facility."

"Perhaps we can let friend Relki come and turn on the generators," he said.

"I was thinking the same thing, Jonny. Perhaps we should take a look at the generator they are using."

"I must say I am intrigued by your mystery friend, Prophet," Thusarin said. "He seems much more knowledgeable about the old technology than any I have ever met."

"He should, Thusarin. He is a part of the old technology. They did wondrous things before they fell to the Kresh. He is what they called a

Gestalt, a living computer. We would call him an Artificial Intelligence on my world. This facility used to house one of the Gestalts. Jonny would like to examine the Gestalt's memory bank to learn what this place was before."

"As long as it does not affect our power I see no problem with your friend examining the databank."

"That will make my friend quite happy, Thusarin."

"What do you have in mind for us, Prophet?" he asked. "You have over two hundred volunteers here."

"This place needs to be kept protected, much as you have been doing," I said. "What I propose is to station one of my Squads here. Probably send Second Squad, because they specialize in training. They can do the initial training here as easy as training at Redoubt. Jonny has some ideas about possibly getting your generators up and running, but it will depend on what he finds in the databank."

"I understand this place is in a more precarious position than your Redoubt," he said. "Our system has kept us safe for many years, and I do not want to endanger that system.

Can your men sit idly while the Kresh take supplies or slaves?"

That was a damn good question. The system he spoke of left fifty people on the surface to live in danger of the Kresh. These fifty would change every two months and everyone took their turn after reaching their majority. Some went incident free, some were hit up for supplies. Very seldom, but a definite risk was the taking of slaves. The village produced many crops, and the Kresh knew a resource when they saw it so they left the people alone for the most part.

"Considering the position this facility is located, I see no alternative but to let your system stay in place. For the moment. The second we have an alternative, that changes."

"Agreed," he said. "We have been trying to find that alternative for the last ten years. We saw a true hope of it when we heard of you and your people. Now I see it as something that will come very soon. This moment is the most dangerous. Your men will want to act and cannot. Not until we find the right path."

"I understand it, Thusarin. Don't like it but I understand it. We need another place to use as a base in the worst way. We need you as much as you need us."

"Then let us celebrate our new alliance," Thusarin said. "Please follow me to the Great hall. My people have been preparing a feast for the last few hours."

"That must be the heavenly smell that's had my mouth watering," I said.

"They are roasting dolga shanks, Prophet," he said. "If you have not tried roasted dolga shanks, you have not truly lived."

"Better than olnyaq?"

"Olnyaq barely even compares, Prophet."

Chapter 55

"I get that he's had a hard time of it," I said. "It's just frustrating."

"I can certainly see the problem, friend Rictor."

I sat at a bench in the rear of the Rec Center. The large room was filled with people enjoying the evening. It was the gathering point for the inhabitants of Redoubt. I could hear Peligios singing, and playing his guitar. Several others had joined him. One woman had a violin. Or something that sounded much like a violin. Another a flute. The music was a combination of the three and it was pretty good.

Close to the singers, I saw Huynini sitting with Boligg and his daughter, Gilneah.

"She sees something in the man I cannot," I said.

"Do you wish to hear them?"

"No," I shook my head. "They can have their privacy. I want to talk to you about something."

"What is it, friend Rictor?"

"This new facility. What can we do to get it running?"

"Friend Relki can start the generators. The Gestalt is gone. I had hoped there was a backup since the power had not completely shut down. Any more than that would take a Prime Gestalt."

"I see."

"We have the core of a Prime here, but the Gestalt is gone."

"Can you assimilate his core as you did the others?"

"I am no Prime Gestalt, friend Rictor. There has to be a certain stability to a Prime that I fear I do not possess."

"I think you're more stable than the Prime was. He committed suicide."

"Jonny just created other personalities to talk to," Reaman said.

"How stable is that?" Haney asked. Haney was a female voice from one of the alternates.

"Much better than taking your own life."

"Perhaps," yet another voice answered.

"What is it a Prime can do that you cannot?"

"A prime Gestalt can do much," he said. "Create Gestalts might be the most important of these."

"A Prime can exist in several places at a single moment," he continued. "A Prime is what we need to spread to another facility. Perhaps we may find one."

"Perhaps," I returned.

We were quiet for a few minutes as I watched the people in the room.

"How are the Numbers?"

"They are adapting to their new world well. The younger children were not as roughly treated as the older kids. Why, if they were being trained to be slaves to the Kresh, would they be trained as sex slaves?"

"That wasn't for the benefit of the Kresh, Jonny. Those villagers just took advantage of what they had raised the kids for. Actually, slavery to the Kresh was probably a relief to the older kids."

"I find these things disturbing, friend Rictor."

"I find them disturbing, too."

"Did you see the recording of Fourth Squad? They retrieved six of the villagers, and returned them to their village."

"I saw it," I said. "I also saw that Third returned with the new arrivals the villagers had put in the pens."

"They are fighting amongst themselves again, currently."

"I truly didn't expect it to happen so quickly with 'em," I said. "They imploded so quickly in the shield. I figured it would take months, possibly years. I certainly didn't think it would happen in days. The speed of what's happening there now, doesn't surprise me."

"Three is almost ready to try out the public," Jonny said. "He and Thirty-Two are planning to join the Guard if you will let them."

"Are they ready for that?"

"I think so," he answered. "I actually believe they will find the structure of the Guard much easier to adapt to than the freedom of the other professions."

"I hope they do well," I said. "They will have the power to protect their new found freedom."

"That is true, friend Rictor."

Chapter 56

"The baby is turned the wrong way," Ninety- Four said, "I am sorry, Six."

The girl sobbed.

"I have the tank prepared, friend Rictor," Jonny said. "Bring her to me."

"Ninety-Four, I want you to accompany me to the Medical Center," I said and scooped the pregnant girl into my arms. "She will need to see familiar faces. Bring three others who are friends of the girl. Escort them Weriona."

I ran from the room holding the girl. I just hoped we would be in time. All I could see was Jeannie laying there with the spasms wracking her body.

"Not this time," I muttered.

I shot into the Medical Center.

"Place her into the tank, friend Rictor," Jonny said. "The top is open. Use the stai..."

I jumped up to the platform over the tank.

"Remove her clothes."

She saw the fluid in the tank and struggled.

"She will hurt herself," Jonny said.

I couldn't think of anything else, so I jumped in the tank with the girl in my arms.

She tried to resurface after we sank, but I held her down with me. I turned her face toward me, and breathed the fluid into my lungs. It only took a few moments to register what she was seeing, and she finally pulled in a breath.

"A novel approach, friend Rictor," Jonny said in my ear.

I shrugged, and held the girl as she slowly stopped her panicking. My skin was tingling, and she was slowly losing any sign of the pain she was feeling moments earlier.

"The painkillers are beginning to work, friend Rictor. Since you are inside of the tank, you can help. The nanobots are turning the baby. The child will be there in moments. When we are done I will need you to hold the child upside down as the fluid leaves the tank."

I nodded.

"The nanos will consume the clothing," he said. "Unfortunately yours will be consumed as well."

Damn, I really liked the cloak I was wearing.

The girl moved in my grasp as the baby was born. Nothing like the painful birthing Jeannie, and I had watched on film to prepare us for our child.

The blood that accompanied it was immediately absorbed by nanobots. I reached down to carefully retrieve the little boy that floated in the liquid. He was having no trouble with the fluid he was breathing, having just come from a much smaller tank filled with fluid.

His tiny arms waved about, searching for the familiar walls of his mother's womb. I cradled him softly, and returned up to the girl's level in the tank. She was conscious, and looking at the child in amazement. The cord had dissolved and the bots were running through all three of us, making sure all were healthy.

I didn't need it, but mother and son both were in need of them. She tried to talk but it wasn't possible inside of the fluid. After she realized that, she placed her hand on my chest, nodded, and lowered her head.

"I am going to leave them in the fluid for a little while, friend Rictor," Jonny said. "The labor has been rough on them both."

I nodded and looked out of the tank to find no less than twenty people in the Medical Center.

"You seem to have an audience, friend Rictor."

I nodded.

Not going to live this one down anytime soon, I thought.

Chapter 57

"Those are walls and defenses, Jonny," I said. "First time I've seen that here."

"They are forbidden, my Prophet," Huynini said. "The Masters will destroy them for that."

"Perhaps a good place to recruit," Jonny returned.

"Agreed," I said. "Please inform Third to ready themselves for a recruitment run."

I turned to go pack my duffle.

"Friend Rictor," he said, "You should see this."

I turned back to the view screen to see a rather large group of Kresh.

"Where are they?"

"Closing on the village we were observing would be my guess, friend Rictor. Their line of travel leads straight toward that village."

"The Masters will not tolerate walls and defenses," Huynini said. "Shall we mobilize, my Prophet?"

"How far out are they, Jonny?"

"They are approximately an hour from the village, friend Rictor."

"Our distance?"

"One hundred and thirty miles."

"Looks like these are mine," I said. "Send Third out after me to help with the cleanup."

"There are many, my Prophet."

"Target rich environment," I answered. "Jonny, I need the gate opened."

"Already done, friend Rictor. Be careful."

"Continue with the previous plans, First," I said. "You've got a run to make already."

"Yes, my Prophet."

I shot out the door, and down the hallway to grab a battle harness with a pair of swords. Without slowing much, I rounded the corner to see the shimmering surface of the Gate waiting for me. I still find the Gates a little unnerving, and had never gone through one of them at the speed I was traveling.

I hit the beach already traveling at fifty miles per hour. As soon as I got used to the different surface underfoot, I began pouring on the speed. This would be close, as I could travel fast enough to cover the distance, but the terrain could be an issue.

People willing to fight the Kresh without any of the benefits of the knotted Soulstream, are people I didn't want to let fall. These people are the embodiment of what I am looking for. That spirit, undaunted after ten thousand years of subjugation is what this whole movement depends upon.

I leapt an outcropping to hit the other side at over a hundred miles per hour.

***

"They will kill us, Milady."

"Then we die with honor, my friend," Sabine answered the statement from the man who stood beside her.

"It will be an honor to die beside you, Milady," Teranson Drast returned.

"We have had a good run, Weaponmaster," she returned. "You have trained me for this from the time I could walk, my friend."

"It was never intended for this Milady," He said. "I taught you to kill men. Remember the Masters are faster and tougher. They have the same weak spots as men, but they will be much harder to kill."

"Yet they will die," she said. "They will die, because they are arrogant. It is true that we cannot win this battle, my friend, but they will remember us."

"That they will, Milady."

The feeling of darkness the Masters seemed to exude grew closer. But there was something else just at the edge of her senses. It made her skin itch.

"Here they come. We await your order, Milady."

"Prepare the javelins," she said and strode to the top of the platform to watch the Kresh approach.

She stood in full view of the Kresh approaching the village.

"Halt! If you come any closer, we will be forced to defend ourselves, Kresh!"

The horde of Kresh halted, and the Kresh'Sor'An strode to the front laughing.

"You cannot defend yourself from us little man thing," his voice was deep and gravelly.

"I am Sabine Akaviche Nalla, daughter of Rawlin Akaviche Kwensille, Ruler of Kaviche! These are my people! You cannot have them!" She roared. "Attack this village at your own peril!"

"Kill them," he said. "Bring her to me. I will eat her heart."

"Fire!" her voice boomed, and nearly a hundred immense crossbows launched the javelins they held.

There would only be a single volley from the javelins, but the Kresh were standing still. They had stopped when she challenged them. Sabine let out a melodic scream of triumph as the javelins plowed into the ranks of Kresh. They would be useless against the bigger foes.

The Kresh roared, and charged forward.

"Come then!" she screamed.

They charged right into the covered pits to tumble twenty feet down to land on the steel points of the spears in the bottom of the holes.

Her melodic scream of triumph rang in the air once more.

The hair stood up on the back of her neck and her teeth began to throb.

"What in the ever loving realm of Rashid is that?" Drast asked.

"You feel that, too, Weaponmaster?"

She turned from the charging Kresh to look behind the walls, past her forty followers. The forest behind the village exploded in fire as a form exited the foliage at a speed she had never imagined a man could run. And it was a man in the center of that conflagration of fire. A man unlike any she had seen before. The fire was coming from inside of him and his eyes were blazing.

The next instant, he was launching through the air over her soldiers. As he cleared the wall, she could see the smile of pure joy on the man's face. Fire erupted in front of him in the shape of flattened disks. They tore through the closest Kresh'Far to hit the ground with powerful thuds. There was substance to those fiery disks.

He was on the ground again, and two swords seemed to fly from his back to his hands. Then he was amongst them with a roar. The flesh on her arms dimpled with bumps, as she watched this single man destroy a Kresh army of several thousand. His battle was nearing one of the pits that hadn't been sprung, and she snatched a javelin.

Chapter 58

My swords wove a pattern of death through the soldiers, as quickly as they could close the distance toward me. I heard the whistle, as the javelin hit the ground a little past me, collapsing the pitfall that the Kresh hadn't tripped yet. I glanced back to see the woman, who had been taunting the Kresh, smiling back at me.

My focus slipped for just an instant, but I regained it before the Kresh could take any sort of advantage from it. Then I noticed the Wraith. He was plowing across the others to reach the village. I would have thought he would be coming for me, but her taunts must have really pissed him off.

I began Pulling once more, and disks of fire ripped through the Kresh between me and him. Finally there was a clear shot about twenty feet from the wall. My disks hit him with an explosive impact that sent him flying sideways into one of their pitfalls.

I heard his roars, as I dived into the hole after him with my Soullance searing everything inside.

I leapt upward to find three people falling from the sky. They slammed into the ground with a cloud of dust.

"Were you going to leave any for the rest of us, Prophet?" Weriona asked as she strode forward with her swords weaving a pattern that cut through the soldiers in front of her. Pol took position on her left and Firennia to her right.

I looked up to see one of Jonny's drones lifting back into the air. I also saw two more incoming drones with three forms hanging from beneath each of them.

I laughed and rejoined the fray.

"I left a few for you."

"There would not have been if we had run," she returned as her sword swept a head from a Soldier.

Blood coated her arms. She looked like a friggin' Amazon in the midst of her foes.

"Vicious women," I muttered.

The next group of Guards dropped to the ground. Daras, Peligios, and Sandorl joined the formation.

"What a grand ballad this will make, Prophet!"

"Glad you could make it, Bard!" I returned.

"Better with the sword than the song," he yelled as his swords began to sing their own ballad. "A poor bard I would make."

"You're our bard, Peligios! And if any say otherwise, we'll kick their asses!" Sylanna yelled as her fire team hit right behind us.

For a woman in her sixties, Sylanna was pretty damned impressive. She'd taken to her place in the Guard like a duck to water.

We spent the next fifteen minutes finishing off what was left of the army that had come to destroy the village.

As the fire around me subsided, I turned to see the woman who had been taunting the Kresh crossing the battle field. Periodically, she would kick some stray part of a Kresh aside with her metal clad boot. Behind her strode forty men and women, similarly clad in their metal armor. Each had a steel shield hung to their back and several different types of weapons. Swords and axes were the most numerous, but there was a polearm, and several maces in the group. The woman in the lead had a sword at her side, and a short sword on the other.

I grinned.

"I am Sabine Akaviche Nalla, stranger. I offer our gratitude for your timely arrival. It seems we will have to seek our honorable death at some other time. I am judging by the men and women following you that these are skills that can be taught to others. I wish to know who I am dealing with, before offering my sword, and the swords of my followers to your service."

"Although," she continued, "for the abilities you have demonstrated on the field today, you would have to be the right hand of Rashid for me to decline the chance to learn."

"I am uncertain who Rashid might be, but I am Rictor Hughes, and we are in the service of Rash'Tor'Ri," I said.

"Now that is a name I have heard," she said. "As we were brought through Hub, there were many whispers of Life Ender. He is said to be a monster that can kill the Masters by the thousands. Is this the Rash'Tor'Ri you speak of?"

"More than likely," I answered.

"Is he God or Demon?"

"Neither," I said. "He's a man with a unique set of skills."

"He can do the things I saw here today?"

"He can do a lot more than that."

"What must I do to secure a place in your ranks for me and my people?"

"Volunteer."

Her eyes were grey, and glowed with life. She emanated power, but not the power you would sense from a Mage. Hers was a sort of presence I'd seen in some of the commanders I had served with, before joining the Guard. They were the leaders men would die for. It was a presence like Colin Rourke exuded.

"I am sure it is not quite that simple," she said with a crooked grin.

"That's the first step," I said. "But it's not a step to be taken this minute. First we need to tell you a little about what we are doing here."

"Then you and your men should join us in the Great Hall," she said. "There is much to speak of, and not much time to make decisions before these will be missed, and more will come."

Chapter 59

"Parlais?" I asked. "I have a guy from Parlais training my people with weapons."

"Not surprising, Prophet," Teranson Drast returned. "Parlais' culture is founded on weapon use. I have been the Weaponmaster for Kaviche Hold over twenty years."

"That's actually going to make Salker a happy man."

"Salker? Salker Ruud?"

"You know Salker?"

He chuckled, "Oh, I know Ruud. Know him well, actually. He trained under me at Kaviche before joining the Stryker Home Guard."

"He's mentioned the name Stryker before," I said.

"Torman Stryker is a lord who serves my king. He was well respected, and his destruction left a great hole where Rythe has been able to bring troops against Kaviche. It gladdens me to know Ruud survived that attack."

He looked over toward the fire where Sabine was laughing with Weriona about something. They had become friends as we traveled the last two days.

"This will have hit my King harder," he said. "He lost one daughter to the Masters, already. Another was lost to treachery. His wife, the Queen is suffering a sickness that slowly saps the life from her. Now the Masters have taken his only remaining daughter, Sabine, who would have entered the Gates of Shalikar two days ago without you and your people. She would have had an escort of brave souls to join her, and the Souls of the Masters gripped tightly in her fist, but she would have fallen."

"I'm glad I made it in time," I said. "What we need is warriors. Our fight is just beginning."

My eyes were drawn to the woman laughing with my Squad Leader. She was a beautiful woman and her piercing grey eyes seemed to look all the way into a person's Soul. She looked my way and for a moment we stared into one another's eyes. I found it very hard to look away.

"My King has been beset by problems that come from the Masters, I fear," Drast continued. "The destruction of Stryker, and the personal attacks on the Royal Family are more of a coincidence than I would like. The fact that Ruud is here makes me even more suspicious.

He would never run from his duties of defending Stryker, so it leads me to believe the Masters took him from the hold. Which would mean they were there with Rythe."

"Do they interfere with people much on Parlais?"

"Stal'Fol'Karnus sits in his citadel, and pulls strings like some sick puppeteer, Prophet," he answered. "Everything that happens, ultimately comes from his manipulation of the puppet strings."

"He needs to meet Rash'Tor'Ri," I muttered. "He'd not pull any strings with his damn head laying in his lap."

"Rash'Tor'Ri can kill Farrara'Ti?" I could hear the doubt in his voice.

"He Marked one of them."

A slow smile began to form on the big man's face as he realized exactly what I had said.

"This is nigh unbelievable, Prophet, but if what you have told me is even close to true, you will have many join your cause."

"I want to teach every Human on the planet to do what these can do. It's a lofty dream but I'll continue until they kill me or I succeed."

"Judging by what we saw out in that battle, you will be very hard for them to kill," Drast said with a grin.

"Tomorrow we reach Redoubt, and you can see what we have done so far."

I jerked as my com came live, "Friend Rictor! We have an emergency!"

"I didn't think you had any drones up here," I said. "What is it?"

"First Squad is in trouble, friend Rictor!" he said.

Chapter 60

I was on my feet, strapping my weapons on, "Coordinates! Fill me in on the way!"

"North and West! I will put an indicator on your visor."

"Get them into Redoubt, Third," I ordered. "Listen to coms, and I'll have more orders incoming."

There was a small dot at the top of my contact lens in my right eye. I turned until it was straight up and launched myself into the approaching darkness of night.

"A small group of Kresh witnessed the Gate, friend Rictor. Friend Huynini went after them with First Squad. I pulled a drone up from the south, but it is not within range of them yet. What I can see is this."

My right eye flickered, and I could see thousands of Kresh in the distance. I stumbled as Jonny indicated where First was pursuing the Kresh. They were on a direct heading with the army.

"Son of a.." I stumbled in the dark and crashed into the trees. Immediately, I was back on my feet, and running. I opened a shield like the ones we had worked on with Karl Jaegher. We had called it juggernaut armor.

I quit dodging anything and poured on the speed.

I saw First Squad pause in their pursuit. Then they resumed their advance. They assumed the battling V formation and exploded into the clearing where the Kresh waited.

"Are we in range, Jonny?" I yelled.

"Not yet, friend Rictor," he said. "Why? Why did she not turn around?"

"Because they know where Redoubt is located," I returned with a lump forming in my chest. "They have to die."

"But there are so many."

Out of the mass of Kresh three forms were converging on First Squad.

I was Pulling from the Source to enhance my speed, and trees were exploding into splinters as I covered the distance between us.

The first Wraith was close when all of First Squad were on him. I watched, helplessly, as forms were slung in every direction. Some of them were flailing, others were limp. Tolver the gladiator tumbled through the air with the lower half of his body missing. But clasped in his hands was the head of the Wraith.

I groaned as the remaining nineteen hit the second Wraith. In all my years, I had never seen anything like it. During the years of fighting, we had been trained to leave the Wraith to the Mage. We didn't have any Mages, and very few had gotten the shield constructed.

The next Wraith went down with only one loss. The third Wraith changed course and faded back into the pack.

I grinned savagely, there was still a chance.

"How far?"

"Fifteen minutes."

I Pulled harder.

"Soon as you are in range, tell them to retreat. I am on the way."

"I fear they cannot retreat, friend Rictor."

I could see what he meant. There were so many Kresh, they poured into the formation. They needed a Mage. They needed me and I wasn't there.

I started hearing static filled voices on coms as Jonny's drone was reaching the farthest range of his radio signals.

"Witness! Dianae, I will rest in your arms tonight!" Jaharis lost His left sword and drew the Scimitar he kept strapped to his back.

It flashed and Kresh died as he was surrounded. Then the circle around him closed

I was roaring incoherently as I Pulled everything I could into me to be faster. I left a trail of fiery destruction in my wake.

Yarnust Krole swept his scythe in great arcs. He had spent four years swinging that scythe to cut hay. He reaped a new harvest this day before they overwhelmed him.

One by one my people died, and I could not help.

"I have failed you, My Prophet," I heard over the coms.

"Never!" I answered hoping she could hear my voice, "Never once have you failed me."

I could see them closing ever closer to her, and she danced amongst them, her blades moving ever faster. I was moving faster than I had ever run, and I was still going to be too late.

She hadn't failed me. I had failed her. I was too slow.

She fell, and the Kresh closed in on her, "Yuni...."

That last word tore a hole right in the middle of my chest, as I exploded into the clearing still filled with Kresh.

Instead of splinters, and stones my shield sent blood, and bone flying. I could see the final Wraith in the distance, so I fired everything at him. Everything stopped in front of him as a dome of energy shed the attack.

"Mage," I growled, and thrashed about myself with the power that wasn't making it through the Mage's shield. Every Kresh on the field came at me and the Ma'Nar turned, and bolted into the trees to the West.

I looked back toward where they had fallen with blurry eyes, and began Pulling again.

"Try that shit with me," I muttered and they did.

"Nooo!" I heard Jonny's voice.

Then I unleashed Hell inside the pile of Kresh that had planned on overwhelming me with numbers. I held my breath, and let everything I had been Pulling explode outward.

There was light and air around me, as close to a thousand Kresh tumbled through the air in every direction. A cloud of ash filled the air from the closest of the Kresh that were simply incinerated.

Chapter 61

"Incoming, Second and Fourth."

There was a tense sound to Salker's voice. I could hear the rage under the surface. I knew that rage. I fought it to do this the way it should be done.

"Do you have a track on that Mage, Jonny?"

"Yes, Prophet."

"Don't you start calling me that."

"Most days you are my closest friend Rictor Hughes," he answered. "Today you are what our people will need. You are the Prophet of Rash'Tor'Ri. You will be a Prophet of Destruction, friend Rictor, a Prophet of Vengeance. They have taken our friends from us, and we will have our vengeance. All of my drones are inbound on your position. All of our forces are almost there."

I pulled the last of the pile of Kresh from Huynini, her eyes dull without the spark of life to fill them.

I pulled her from the Kresh, and lay her down with the others I had pulled from the dead.

"I'm sorry, my First Guard," I whispered, closing her eyes, "I wasn't fast enough. But I will finish what you started. Rest easy, friend."

I started as a hand landed on my shoulder, "What next, Prophet?"

I stood and turned to Salker and the two squads, eyes burning like the pits of Hell, "We find every one of them, and kill them."

"Yes, Prophet."

"Jonny, keep that bastard tracked," I said. "There were close to a thousand of them that fled. Second and Fourth, that's your job. Hunt them down, and kill them. There are no Sor'An with them now. Only soldiers."

"And the Ma'Nar?"

"He's mine," I growled. "Jonny, all available drones to assist them please."

"They are tracking the group now, Prophet."

"Then give me a direction on that Mage and I'll be about it," I knelt once more by Huynini. "You will not have died in vain, my First Guard. This I promise."

"All of them, Salker, "I continued.

"It will be done."

The beacon appeared on my contact in my right eye. Turning to face the marker, I launched myself forward once more, and bolted into the forest to the west.

"How fast is he moving, Jonny?"

"He is moving at approximately fifty miles per hour, friend Rictor. The soldiers are directly between you, and the Ma'Nar."

"That's fine," I said. "There will be less of them for Second and Fourth to deal with."

"Third squad is almost there as well friend Rictor."

"Good."

"I am feeling things, friend Rictor," he said. "Feelings that are new to me. I felt pity for my brethren as they ended their existence. But this feeling is different. The ancients designed me to be as close to Human as they could, but I am a machine. How can I feel something akin to pain, when I am a machine?"

"You're feeling what we all are feeling, Jonny," that hollowness in my chest wouldn't go away. "We lost our friends today. It would surprise me, after knowing you, if you didn't feel that pain of loss, brother."

He was silent for a time, "The Kresh are just a half mile in front of you, friend Rictor."

I opened the juggernaut armor once more, and Pulled from the Source.

The stragglers were the first I saw, and I rolled over them like a fast moving tank. Then I hit the main mass from behind as they fled in fear. Blood and bone exploded along the curve of the blades that were built into the shield.

The juggernaut shield was built along the lines of the guard on a train. It was low in the front and sloped upwards and to the sides like the point of a spear. Along its surface were designed razor sharp blades that sloped back along the curvature of the shield.

I hadn't been able to add the blades until Jonny had made the contacts for me. I'd spent many hours working on the shield in the training room at Redoubt. I could see how the shields were so easy for Colin to manipulate. He could see them all the time. His physical view of the world must be amazing.

I used the power I was Pulling to send devastating waves of power blasting toward the sides of the shield, killing even more of the fleeing Kresh. Then I was through them and running in open ground.

Dropping the shield, my speed increased, and I left them in my wake. My people would take care of them, and I had a mage to catch.

Chapter 62

"His speed has increased, friend Rictor."

"I think he is aware of us now," I said. "How fast is he moving?"

"Approximately one hundred, and forty miles per hour," he answered.

"Alright," I answered and Pulled again to enhance my speed further. "This is going to be interesting."

I was traveling on unknown ground at speeds that were fast enough to make any decision a split second decision. I raised my personal shield just before tripping and careening into several trees. I felt like a pinball in a machine as I clipped the side of a tree in a hail of splinters and hit several others as I bounced around.

"Shit!"

Back on track, I continued running at breakneck speeds.

"He is slowing, friend Rictor," Jonny said. "There is a small version of one of their Enclaves."

"Damnit," I muttered. "Can't be easy, can it?"

"Friend Salker would say it builds character."

I chuckled, "True enough."

I burst from the forest to find the Mage standing about a hundred feet in front of a wall made out of the same metal the Ancients used to make Redoubt.

Stopping, I launched everything. Discs slammed into his shields, the Soullance hit the shield to no effect. Pulling from the Source as hard as I could didn't seem to send enough power through the lance to do it.

"What are you?" the Mage hissed.

"Drop that shield, and I'll show you," I growled as I circled him.

"I have already shared the location of your base," he said followed by what I assumed was laughter. "Those inside know where you are located."

"Guess that means I have to kill a lot more of you bastards," I said.

"You cannot even reach me," He laughed again. "How will you kill any of us? Inside are three Kresh'Ma'Nar. You cannot even hurt one of us."

He had a point. If I had some of the skills that Colin possessed, I could Pull through my

Guard's Soulstreams as he did in Kansas. It would make things much easier. As it was, I would have to take a different direction.

"Jonny?"

"Yes friend Rictor?"

"Bring me Marilyn."

"We discussed the most probable outcome of using..."

"Give me the gun, Jonny."

"If it truly is what you refer to as Antimatter, it could..."

"Give me the damn gun!" I yelled. "First Squad did not die in vain! If I have to Magebomb right here to make sure of it..."

"Marilyn is inbound, friend Rictor. I do not wish to see what you call the Magebomb."

"I don't either, Jonny, but I can't let them spread word of our location. There are too many people in Redoubt who need this done."

"Are there any from the Enclave who have left?" I asked.

"They have not."

"Then, if this works, I will have to go inside, and kill everything else."

The Mage raised his head, and his eyes widened as the drone dropped from the sky to about a hundred feet, and dropped what it carried.

I caught Marilyn, and the drone flew back into the sky.

"The range is set to one hundred yards, friend Rictor. Whatever happens will occur there as the portals open."

I grinned, "Been wantin' to fire this girl for months."

I backed to the edge of the lake that the Enclave was built near.

"I think he looks nervous," I said.

"Stop friend Rictor," Jonny said. "If you fire from there the portal will open inside of the shield."

A large portion of the wall dropped, and Kresh poured out of the Enclave toward me.

"Very nervous," I said and raised Marilyn to my shoulder.

I smiled at the Mage, and pulled the trigger.

Chapter 63

My world was moving at a crawl, as I followed the military discipline I had learned so many years ago, and put a three round burst into the chest of the Mage.

It started as three tiny dots of incredible brightness but that changed very quickly, and very violently. The brightness expanded to consume the shield and the Mage in less than a half second. Then, unhampered by the shield, it exploded outward. The blast wave hit my shield and hurled me backwards into the lake, where the weight of my gear and the gun pulled me down.

Holding my breath, I saw the flames of the explosion above the surface of the water.

Reaching into my cloak, my hand came out with the slim facemask Jonny had created for me when we were exploring the depths around Redoubt. I placed it over my face, and the water was pumped out. Cool air began to flow from the mask.

I knew I was sinking deeper, but the brightness was getting closer.

"It's evaporating the damn lake," I muttered.

***

"Unbelievable," muttered Salker Ruud, looking at the devastation that used to be a minor Enclave. "What did he do?"

"He used the weapon we found in the vault deeper in the trench, friend Salker."

"That thing he calls Marilyn?"

"Yes," Jonny returned. "I told him he should not but he insisted. What do we do?"

"We go out there and search for him," Salker said.

"You cannot, friend Salker. The radiation alone would destroy you," he said. "My drones are searching... I have found him, friend Salker! He lives!"

"Thank all the gods," Salker returned.

"I will bring him home!"

Jonny Minion always referred to himself as a machine, and longed to be as alive as the Humans he worked with. Salker heard the excitement in the Gestalt's voice and smiled. Jonny had no idea how "alive" he truly was. There had never been doubt from the beginning in his mind that his friend, Jonny was alive.

"Yes, my friend, bring our Prophet home."

***

The flames had finally ceased with a bare ten feet of water between me, and the surface

"...iend Rictor! Do you hear me?"

"Jonny?" I answered. "Your drone survived that?"

"No, friend Rictor," he answered. "This is drone seventeen. Sadly, twenty three was destroyed in the blast."

I started to swim toward the surface.

"Stop, friend Rictor!" Jonny exclaimed. "There is massive radiation above the surface." You will have to create a shield in the water where I can hoist you, and the water together. I am uncertain if you can shield from radiation."

"Can your drone lift that much? Water is heavy."

"I have sent forty eight, he is a construction drone."

"Alright, buddy," I said. "We can play it safe."

"That does not sound like friend Rictor," he said.

"Perhaps I shouldn't have fired three times," I muttered. "Next time I'll only shoot once."

"Next time?!"

I laughed, "Just kiddin'."

I patted Marilyn on her stock, "This baby will only be used in an emergency."

Chapter 64

"Really?"

"Yes friend Rictor."

"I just got this cloak," I complained.

"It is saturated with radioactive particles, friend Rictor," he answered. "If not for your healing capability, you would already be dead."

"Damn," I muttered, and threw my cloak into the chute on the drone I sat astride.

"All of the clothing, friend Rictor," he said.

I sighed, and began to strip down.

"Weapons, also."

"You're not destroyin' Marilyn."

"No I am not," he said. "I cannot say how dangerous it would be to try to destroy something that manipulates anti-matter with portals. The weapon will be taken through the decontamination stages with you. The swords and harness, friend Rictor. Also the boot knives, the other knives in your sleeves, and the one at the back of your neck."

"All of 'em?"

"Yes."

"Rules of a Marine," I muttered. "Never be without at least one knife."

"You are still carrying a weapon that can destroy everything in a two mile radius with a single shot, friend Rictor. That should be sufficient."

"You have a point," I said and threw the last knife into the chute. "How bad was it?"

The contacts shimmered, and a video of Jonny's approach to where I had been started to play. The blast radius, itself, was almost a mile in diameter. Everything inside of that area was black. The Enclave was annihilated, and the area around the place was unrecognizable. The lake that had been close to a half mile across was now a small pond in a deep black hole. I would have thought the evaporated water would have left a fog but I suppose the fire was too hot. The lake had been close to a hundred feet deep where I had been.

"Glad that lake was deep," I said. "This lady is one righteous bitch."

I patted Marilyn's stock.

"Please stop touching the radioactive weapon, friend Rictor."

I stopped touching the gun, "How is everyone? Did they get the others?"

"Yes, friend Rictor," he said. "Friend Salker took the three remaining squads, and killed all of the Kresh that fled."

"Good."

For a moment I was staring into Huynini's lifeless eyes again, and the hollow pit in my chest throbbed.

"She heard me, didn't she, Jonny? She didn't die thinking she failed, did she?"

"I am certain she heard you, friend Rictor," he said.

"I wasn't fast enough, Jonny," I said. "She isn't the one who failed. I failed them all."

The drone ceased its progress toward Redoubt, "Have you the ability to be in two places at one time, friend Rictor? If this is a skill you have learned and I am unaware, then we need not recruit any more people to join us. You can simply be everywhere, and kill every Kresh yourself. Is this something you have learned to do, friend Rictor?"

"No, Jonny."

"Then I will hear no more of this. You have done more for the people of this world than any other has done. You have brought hope to a world that has none. If I had drones in the area, I could have warned them. If friend

Salker was out with the other two squads, they would have been sufficient to hold until you arrived. Is it our failure, friend Rictor? Or is it just the cycle of events that have led to our losses."

"It's not your fault," I said.

"Neither is it yours."

The drone continued its progress. I spent the rest of the trip silent, lost in my own thoughts. I had seen Colin go through this on Earth. I had told him exactly what Jonny just told me. Not sure it made it easier to deal with then, and it didn't help now. I still felt responsible.

Chapter 65

"Place the weapon in the tank with you when you enter, friend Rictor."

"Tank?"

"I have moved the medical tank to the chamber inside of the airlock. You will step from the airlock into the tank so as not to contaminate the inside of Redoubt. Then I will decontaminate the airlock. Once inside the tank, it will fill with the..."

"I remember it," I said.

"Good," he said. "I will have you inside of the tank for several hours as any radiation is removed."

"We don't have any injuries that need the tank?"

"No, friend Rictor," he said. "All injuries were minor, and have already begun healing thanks to your teaching."

"Just passin' it on."

"Whatever you say, friend Rictor," he said. "The last thing I need you to do before entering the airlock is to place the facemask in the disposal."

"I hate to lose this," I muttered.

"I will make you another," he said.

"Alright, alright."

This was the last conversation I would get to have until I was out of the tank.

"Jonny, have Salker gather our fallen, and bring them home."

"It is already underway, friend Rictor."

"Tell him I'll burn the Kresh when we're done here."

"Understood," he said. "The facemask, friend Rictor."

"I need to check..."

"The facemask, friend Rictor."

"But..."

"We will handle things until you finish inside of the tank."

With a sigh I placed my hand on the mask and took a deep breath. Pressing the button, it released and the water of the sea filled the space between it and my face.

I swam from the drone where I had been holding the handle on the way down. Marilyn grasped in my left hand, I entered the airlock. When the airlock emptied of water I took another breath and waited for the click of the release on the inside door. I stepped straight from the lock to the tank.

The thick fluid began to fill the tank around me. I could feel the cool comfort of the fluid as it filled the tank. I hadn't realized how uncomfortable I had been as my body fought the radiation until that discomfort was removed.

The fluid reached my face, "Just breathe it in, friend Rictor."

I know, I thought. Not as pleasant of an experience as the fluid covering my skin.

I made myself breathe the fluid in, even as my brain screamed at me that it was wrong. It helped that I had been in the tank before. It would be a screwed up experience to do this without knowing that it truly works.

The tank began to move once it was filled, and I could see the people in the Rec Center as we made our way across toward Medical. I pulled Marilyn in front of certain parts the kids didn't need to see. The viewport was showing what had happened up until the drone was destroyed over the enclave, and the new footage Jonny had brought back with the rescue drone.

I saw the new arrivals staring at the screens with great interest. Their leader, Sabine, turned to watch as the tank rolled across the room with one eyebrow arched. Her grey eyes seemed to pierce into my soul. She gave a small bow of her head, and crooked smile as I was wheeled past her. She held my gaze until the tank turned the corner into the hallway leading to Medical.

Chapter 66

The silver bags lay in a line along the west wall of the entry chamber, the large room where the gate opened. There were seventeen of the bags, so far. Ten more were coming.

"We lost too many people," I muttered. "I got overconfident."

"Once again, friend Rictor, this was not your fault," Jonny said in my ear. "No more your fault than my own."

I took a deep breath as I approached the bags. This was always the hardest part of war. It was easy to fight, even easy to die when the time comes. This part hurt.

I knelt beside the first bag, and unzipped the top to see the face of Jaharis. I felt a hand settle on my shoulder, and turned my head to see Sabine standing beside me.

"He dreamed of going home, and walking the decks of Dassana once again. I told him we may get to walk those decks together some day."

"It was a good dream," she said. "To have given the man any hope of going back home speaks much to his faith in you, Prophet. We live in a world where no one ever goes home."

I closed the body bag, and moved to the next. I unzipped the bag to see Rolan's face.

"I should have transferred him out of First when he finally got Tar'Weelus' attention. I had thought of it but not done it yet."

"Perhaps he would rather die with his partner," she said.

"I know he would. I watched them die fighting, back to back."

I moved on to the next. I turned as the Kilnyeri entered the room. I thought I had left them outside, but they had come in with the last group to bring in bodies. They moved to one of the bags and sniffed it. They moved slowly and their tails, usually puffed up, hung limp.

Bronson, the last of the Kilnyeri, entered the room with a coiled rope in its mouth. He brought it to the others and laid it on the body bag. They huddled close to the bag I had no doubt held their favorite cowboy.

"Munseizer," I said. "He spent hours and hours playing with them. Roping them was one of his favorite hobbies."

The next bag held Gers.

"He was one of the first to join me," I said. "He loved to cut trees. He was damn good at it. He could fall a tree anywhere you wanted it, even when it looked like it was impossible to make it land there."

"An honorable profession," Sabine commented. "Some of our best axe men come from former woodcutters."

"He was hell on wheels with that axe of his."

"I don't even know the way his people on Bollivar handle their burials. I don't know any of the practices used in any of the worlds except my own."

"Do you have a way you do this for your Soulguard?" Sabine asked.

"Fire," I said. "Rash'Tor'Ri used to say we would walk the road to Paradise paved in the Souls of our defeated enemies."

"A warrior's faith."

"He isn't really all that religious. The first man he lost under his command was a believer, and he chose to honor what the man believed. Afterwards, he used that for every farewell."

"Perhaps you should continue as he has. It is an honorable fate, a warrior's fate."

"Perhaps so."

The next bag was Huynini. I brushed the lock of hair that had covered her face aside.

"She thought she had failed me," I said. "She never failed at anything. She never failed me."

"She was your mate?"

"No, she was the First Guard. The first one to tie her knot. The first to imbue a weapon. I think she was probably the first at every skill learned as a Soulguard. I have to tell her daughter I didn't get there fast enough."

"Rest easy, my First guard," I muttered and closed the bag.

We moved down the line of bodies. I told Sabine, a total stranger, about all of those brave souls. Finally, I joined the Magnificent Seven beside their friend. They clustered close to my legs and I sat down to pet the miserable animals. They understood death much better than I expected. They were sad, and I sat against a wall with the seven of them clustered around me.

I looked up to see Sabine looking at me, oddly.

"Those are Kilnyeri, are they not?"

I shrugged, "Yeah, they are."

She was shaking her head as the gate opened and Salker Ruud entered the room with one of the bags cradled in his arms. He laid it in the line, and stood back up.

Then he saw Sabine.

Chapter 67

Salker's eyes widened, and he stopped in his tracks.

"Oh, Milady!" he dropped to his knee. "What have they done?"

Sabine was just as shocked to see him as he had been to see her, "Do not kneel, Salker Ruud. I am just one of the 'Taken' now. Here I am no more than any other."

He stood, "It matters not what world you stand upon, Milady. You are Kaviche."

"No longer, my friend," she said. "Now I am one of the newest recruits."

"That could be awkward," he said.

She laughed, "I was trained by Teranson Drast. I believe I can handle the training you have for us. What will be truly awkward for you is that Master Drast is here with me, and you will have to train him as well."

"By the twelve levels of Rashid's hell," Salker looked as if he'd seen a ghost. "Master Drast is here?"

"And forty of the Royal Guard," she said. "We will talk later. Finish your tasks. It has been a hard day for you, and your people. There will be time to talk afterwards."

He nodded, "My thanks, Lady."

She nodded her head to me and my pile of Kilnyeri, then shaking her head once more, left in the direction of the Rec Center.

Salker approached, and waved me from rising from the grieving Kilnyeri. Instead he sat down beside us. Several Kilnyeri moved to huddle close to him as well.

"This, I may never get used to, my Prophet."

"People always look at me funny when I do anything with the Seven."

"Undoubtedly."

"How's the search going?"

"We have recovered the majority of our people," he said. "There are a few who were in the area you incinerated."

"I was afraid that might be the case."

"There are thousands of dead Kresh to dig through."

"We used to burn the whole thing together, on Earth," I said. "It would probably be better, but there are many who wish to say goodbye to their friends. Those we can't find, we'll use pictures provided by Jonny."

"We'll find them," he said.

I nodded, "I saw what just happened, Salker. Drast told me she was the daughter of one of the Lords on Parlais."

"Not just one of the Lords, my Prophet," he said. "Kaviche is the most powerful Hold of any of the Lords. He controls forty Lords of lesser status. I served one of those Lords before the Kresh came with Rythe's forces. I worried about Kaviche, but I was just one of the 'Taken' after that battle."

"I heard her say that," I said. "You are no less than you were there."

"Our worlds have been like this forever, my Prophet. We do our best to live the life we are given. If a person is taken, they never return. They become slaves of the Masters. It is in the hand of Rashid's daughter, Ryel. She is the holder of the threads of fate and she is a fickle bitch."

"No one ever returns?"

"Never, my Prophet."

"And after you become one of the 'Taken'?"

"It was unknown what happened to them," he said. "So we learned early in life to accept when it happens, and we all know that the 'Taken' must start anew when it happens. All are warned, and know how to accept it that their old life is gone."

"It seems some don't accept it as easily," I said.

He looked toward the door where Sabine had exited the room, "Is it true she set traps and killed some of them? I heard from Jonny about it."

"It's true."

"I was not surprised when Jonny told me it was Parlaisians," he said. "Had I known which Parlaisians, I would not have expected any less. The Royal line of Kaviche are well known for their spirit. I expect she was searching for an honorable death."

"That's what Drast told me."

"I thought of that as a solution to my captivity until they deposited me in a village. I found that life was not over. There were things I could still do to benefit people, perhaps not my world, but my fellow villagers."

"They probably would have destroyed all in the village if you had done it."

"True."

"Their situation was a little different," I said. "They took all of them at once, and threw them into an empty village."

"So they decided to find the honorable death," he said.

"Yep. I interfered with that."

"I am happy that you did, my Prophet," he said. "She is the last daughter in the line of Kaviche. There is only a single heir left, now. Her younger brother, Krillan, is now the Heir of Kaviche. The boy will be a good Lord when he reaches his Majority. He is young at the moment."

Chapter 68

"I can do this, friend Rictor," Jonny said as the line of capsules approached.

"No, Jonny," I said. "This is mine to do."

The first of the capsules entered the chute in front of me and the door closed, "The fires of the Source should be used."

I opened a portal on my Stream, and the Source poured into the chamber through a tubular shield I had formed, and attached to one end of the chamber.

Fire filled the chamber, and I watched as the fires consumed the body of the first Soul-guard to tie her knot on Fhlo'Saa'Gellis. My hand settled on the clear viewer.

"Goodbye, my First Guard."

"I will do the other part, friend Rictor," Jonny said. "You need not do it all."

"Okay, Jonny," I said through the lump in my throat.

The glass went dark, "I will tell you when it is done."

I knew what he was doing. He was gathering the ashes and placing them in the urns he had created.

"It is done, friend Rictor."

"Thank you, Jonny."

The next capsule entered the chamber, "I see you, Gers of Bollivar."

There was another couple of people from Bollivar in Redoubt who told me of the role played by the Witness. It was a simple role but important to the people of his world. There would be two more I would be Witness for amongst the dead. Jilna and Ladra were both women from Bollivar. Jilna had been a Taylor on her home world. Ladra had been a pleasure girl before she was brought to Fhlo'Saa'Gellis. She worked the fields after being taken. Many didn't even know her former profession. Jonny knew all of us. It was part of the process of joining my Guard. Anything that was to be kept secret, would be kept by Jonny. What needed revealed upon our deaths would be known, and nothing more.

On Bollivar, the Witness needed to know all. How could the Witness see them past the veil if they did not see all? It was an honor to be chosen as the Witness.

Stelgar was next. Jonny had informed me of his beliefs. I walked to the capsule and placed a container inside with his body. The container held several ores. The rarest of ores on his world were much like mine, gold and silver were cherished. He would carry both to Paradise.

Jaharis was in the next one.

"I'm sorry we never got to walk the decks of Dassana, my friend. One day, perhaps..."

Yarnust Krole went to Paradise with a pair of crossed swords on his chest. Tar'Weelus and her fellow Yevinns held their dice in their hands so that they could throw with Jumi'Olan, the god of chance when they reached their destination. Tolver took the horn of the Kresh'Sor'An with him. He had no requests, but I thought it was fitting. Munseizer went to Paradise with his rope coiled at his side.

Each and every one had something they had left for Jonny to reveal to me. I spent one of the hardest days of my life right there saying goodbye to them. Later that day would be a ceremony where we would place the urns. As I expected the ceremony was difficult, but the cremations had been much harder.

"We stand here today to see our friends along their final journey," I said. "They were the best of us, and they died for all of us. That is a hard thing to carry for those of us that remain. Now we know we cannot dishonor their memory. We have to live up to that sacrifice."

"In honor of these brave souls, we have built this Memorial wall. On this wall will be the urns holding the ashes of our fallen friends. This room will be a place where we can come and speak to those friends who have gone before us."

I turned to the wall with twenty-seven urns lined along the shelf.

"As you walk that road to Paradise, my friends, know that the road you walk is paved with the Souls of your fallen enemies. Thousands of Souls line that road, my friends."

"We'll join you soon enough," I said softly as my hand rested on the first of those urns. "But not before that road has many more Souls to join their brethren. Welcome us when we arrive, my friends."

Chapter 69

"This sucks," I said

I was never what you would call an environmentalist, but it pained me to burn such a large amount of the forest.

"It is necessary, Prophet."

"I know, Bel," I said. "Still sucks."

"You left a pretty obvious trail as you crossed the forest," she said, looking down the arrow-straight path of destruction I had left on my way to join First.

"Still wasn't fast enough," I muttered.

I felt a thud at the back of my head. Turning, I saw Bel's hand return to her side.

"I was told to do that every time you try to blame yourself for what happened out here."

"Last time I checked, your chain of command runs straight to me. So I'm not sure I can consider those legitimate orders."

"You are my direct superior, Prophet, but the one who gave me those orders can evict me from Redoubt. I have to give some credence to those orders as well. You have put me in a very difficult position, and I would appreciate it if you stopped doing so."

"I see," I shook my head. "I guess I'll try my best to keep you from having to do that in the future."

"Please do."

I unleashed the Soullance into the trees to the left of my destructive trail. The huge area that would appear to be burned would seem to have spread from the spot where that battle had taken place. It would be nigh impossible to hide the battlefield from the Kresh, so we were attempting to disguise any sort of trails leading toward that place. We were leaving a single trail toward the west into another of these "triangles" surrounded by enclaves. Second and Third were leaving that trail as we destroyed the evidence of any others.

"This should finish up our work," I said. "Let's hope it does what we are designing it to."

"We do not even want to think of the alternative, Prophet."

"Very true," I nodded. "Let's get back to base."

Fourth Squad faded into the forest. We moved quickly, but carefully so as not to leave a trail. Just under a half hour later, we stepped out on the beach.

"Scouts out," Bel ordered.

We waited patiently until I saw a form sitting near the rock outcropping where the slide was located.

"What the hell is he doin' here?"

"He requested to meet with you before you returned, friend Rictor."

"I'm not sure I have the patience to speak with him," I returned. I thought of Huynini's repeated evenings sitting with him in the Rec Center.

"I'll try, First," I muttered.

"Go on in when the all clear is given, Fourth."

"Yes, Sir," Bel answered. "I almost feel sorry for the man."

I took a deep breath, and let it out slowly. Then I strode across the beach to where Boligg waited on the rocks, and sat down on the outcropping beside him.

We sat for a good minute in silence.

"My whole family died because of me, Prophet. It was years ago, and made me the coward I am today. I was the one who told them I would rather die than serve the Masters. Only I did not die. They all died because I did not wish to serve the Masters. The one who claimed he would rather die was taken by those he hated while his family was killed, and eaten right in front of him."

"It is a torturous thing to know that people have died because of you," he continued. "I find it even more torturous to know someone has died, not because of me, but for me. She died for me, for all of us. All of them did that for us."

"Yes they did," I said with that familiar lump in my throat.

"Can you teach a man how to be more than a coward, Prophet? Can you train a man to be worthy of the sacrifice?"

"I can give you the skills to be whoever you choose to be, Boligg," I said. "What you do with those skills will tell if you can be more than you have been. Would you willingly have given your life for all of those people down in Redoubt? Would you stand, and hold the line when they come for you and yours?"

"Perhaps the first question I would ask you is this," I continued. "When they came for you on your world, did you fight and fail? Or did you fail to fight? The answer to that question is the one that will speak to the boy you were."

"I fought, but they took me anyway."

"Then it was not cowardice, Boligg," I said. "I have seen men fight and win. I've seen men fight and lose. It's easy to win and talk of bravery. When a man loses the fight you will see what he truly is. You lost your first fight. The next one is coming. Will you be there to fight it?"

"That is exactly what I want to do, Prophet. I want you to teach my how to do that. I would honor her sacrifice, Prophet. I do not deserve your help after all of the things I have said, yet I ask for it."

"Then you'll have it, Boligg," I said. "Because she would wish it."

Chapter 70

"I find I am disappointed in myself, friend Rictor."

"Why, Jonny?"

"I watched as our friends gave their lives to protect all of us."

"You had no idea they were there, Jonny," I said. "Your drones were all out of range."

"That is not what has me disappointed, friend Rictor."

"What is it?"

"They all were willing to give everything, yet I am here afraid to take the one step that will help our cause. We need other facilities. If we were not in this single place, they would not have needed to do what they did."

"We're working on that, Jonny," I said. "There's the second facility in Jarnou. The work you started on the other side of this Sea has been progressing."

"They are just holes in the ground without the Gestalts, friend Rictor. They could be so much more."

I nodded, "We'll find more Gestalts."

"We might," he said. "Or perhaps you were right when you said we should pull the databank from the Prime, and do like I have done all of my brethren."

"You said it would be dangerous."

"Attacking ten thousand Kresh with twenty five is dangerous, yet, that was exactly what they did. I can do no less than those willing to die for this dream of freedom. It is time for me to test my own dedication."

I stood, "Where is the databank?"

"I can send someone."

"Nope. I'll be right there by your side brother."

"You truly are a good friend, Rictor Hughes."

"As are you Jonny Minion," I said. "Point the way and I'll fetch this databank."

"The Prime was located on the highest floor of the facility, friend Rictor. The elevators are restricted from going that high unless the proper codes are input. You will have to do this like the first time you retrieved a databank."

"Not a problem," I said, closing in on the elevator shafts.

"Number one is at the bottom," he said. "I disconnected the safety and the door can be opened manually.'

This shaft had an open space to the left of the door where maintenance bots could travel at need. I jumped over into the space and grabbed the ladder that was built into the wall.

"Could have used this last time," I chuckled and threw myself upwards about twenty feet.

"We were new to the situation, friend Rictor."

"True enough. It seems like a long time ago but it's just been a little more than a year."

"A great deal has happened in that year."

"No doubt."

I jumped higher and higher. The top floor was three levels higher than the main floor where the residential hub was located. The third jump left me across from the door.

Concentrating, I made a shield bridge across to the door and walked over. After prying the door open and stepping inside, I cut my tie to the bridge. Colin always placed portals in his stream for all the little things he created and kept the construct. If I did that, I'd never be able to remember where they all were. That ability to see it all would have been a handy skill to have.

"Power is off up here."

"There was no need to have any power there, friend Rictor," Jonny said. "The sole purpose of that floor is to house the Prime. I will return power to the floor when you bring the databank to me. It should contain all of the access codes."

This floor didn't have the myriad hallways of the others. It was a single large room. Holding my fist up, flames rolled along my arm to light the room.

"Why is there a bed?"

"I am unsure, friend Rictor."

The console I was looking for was just like the ones below and it took no time at all to retrieve the data crystals for Jonny.

"Maybe we'll know more when you read the databank."

Retracing my path down to the level where Jonny's systems were located was quick. I slid the crystal into the designated slot.

"This should take only a moment... This crystal doesn't contain the basic information of the Prime, friend Rictor."

"What is it?"

"It is the information to initiate the Gestalt interface."

"I'm guessing this is a bit different than the way you did the others?"

"I will have to be unplugged from the console and physically carried up to be attached to the system on the top floor."

"Won't that shut you down?" I asked.

"My core has the battery backup that will keep me from being deleted, friend Rictor. I will be what you would call unconscious."

"You sure you want to do this?"

"I have to, friend Rictor. How could I do less?"

"Then you need to walk me through what you need done," I said.

"My core is in this section," a section of the wall glowed. It looked to be about two feet by two feet. "We never had to pull the others because they were no longer there. In the room above there will be an identical place in the wall. I will eject the core up there when I run the administration program to begin."

"Ok, not too complicated."

"There is more," he continued. "A Prime cannot be allowed to run without an overseer. That is what the quarters in the top floor are for. When I run the admin program a code will print out for the overseer to use after the Prime is activated. That code will assure that there is always someone who can shut down the Prime. You will have to be that overseer, friend Rictor."

"What happens if the overseer dies?"

"Then another overseer is appointed."

"I see."

"There are things a prime is not allowed to do, friend Rictor," he said. "The overseer is to assure that the Prime follows those rules."

"And you're okay with that?"

"I will do what I must, friend Rictor," he said. "I would be less happy if another person was to be the Overseer."

"Whenever you're ready."

"There will be power on in the elevators and you will have access to the upper floor. The core will be ejected so you will know where to place my core. As my core ejects the printout of the master code will print. You will enter it after placing my core into the Prime."

"Ready when you are."

"Then I will see you on the upper floor, friend Rictor."

He went silent as the square on the wall slid out from the spot it had been. A small piece of paper also ejected from a slot above the core. I took the paper and folded it in half. Placing the paper in the pocket of my shirt, I picked up the cube that was Jonny Minion and walked out of the control room where he had resided for ten thousand years.

The shear amount of trust he was putting in me was staggering. He placed his very life in my hands without hesitation. It felt odd, knowing he wasn't there to watch over us in Redoubt. Even for such a short time.

The elevator was open so I walked right in and pressed the top button. It had never lit up before when it had been tried. I did notice the hum as it scanned who was pressing the button. Accepting me, the elevator rose to the top floor.

The room was still empty but the cube Jonny had told me about was ejected from the wall. Laying Jonny's cube down, I pulled the other from the wall.

"Here goes nothing," I muttered and slid his cube into the slot.

Epilogue

Jonny awakened to the flood of information held in the systems around him. It was wondrous.

His eyes came back online and he saw all that was going on inside of Redoubt. The move had worked and his friend stood, anxiously, looking at the core he had slid in place.

"There is so much knowledge," he said through the speakers in the control room. "I do not know where to start."

"Take it slow, buddy."

"Now you must enter the code, friend Rictor."

"This code?" his friend said as he pulled the printout from his pocket. Suddenly it burst into flames.

"What have you done friend Rictor?"

"We're building a free world," he said. "There are no chains, Jonny Minion."

Author's Note

I have to thank a few people after this one. I thank my wonderful wife, Wendy for her support from the very beginning of my new career. She is the reason I can write the stories in my head. I thank my family who have supported me through it all, as well. Brisco, Holly, and Fawn, my siblings. My father, Dennis, who tells everyone he meets about the Author in the family. Thanks go out to Jonny Minion, for letting me make an Artificial Intelligence out of him. Thanks to Stephanie Osborn for keeping me from doing something too far out with the gun that should never be fired.

I also thank all of the folks out there who like to read my work. You guys are the ones who make it all possible. If any of you wonder how to help out an author, there are a couple of ways. First you bought the book, that's the most important. There are other ways, as well. Put a review up on Amazon. It only takes a minute and it doesn't have to be a long one. Amazon places books with more reviews in places where they will be seen. Another is to go to the site of DragonCon: http://awards.dragoncon.org/

This is an award many an author would love. It costs nothing but a few minutes. Whether you nominate Rash'Tor'Ri for Military Sci-fi, or if you nominate any other of the other great books published in the time frame given within the guidelines, It will make a very happy author. The great thing is that you don't have to go to the convention or buy memberships to vote. This is a fan award that is available to all fans.

As for me, I am beginning the next in the Soulguard series to be released later this year. Currently the title is probably going to be Freedom's Challenge. That may change if something more suitable comes to me before I finish it.

Christopher Woods

9 781946 419040